The Skin Is the Elastic Covering
That Encases the Entire Body

# THE SKIN
# IS THE ELASTIC
# COVERING
# THAT ENCASES
# THE ENTIRE
# BODY

BJØRN RASMUSSEN

Translated from Danish by
MARTIN AITKEN

TWO LINES
PRESS

Originally published as:
*Huden er det elastiske hylster der omgiver hele legemet*
© 2011 Bjørn Rasmussen & Gyldendal, Copenhagen
Published by agreement with the Gyldendal Group Agency
Translation © 2019 by Martin Aitken

Two Lines Press
582 Market Street, Suite 700, San Francisco, CA 94104
www.twolinespress.com

ISBN 978-1-931883-85-6

Cover design by Gabriele Wilson
Cover photo by Michael Turek / Gallery Stock
Typeset by Sloane | Samuel
Printed in the United States of America

Library of Congress Cataloging-in-Publication Data
Names: Rasmussen, Bjørn, 1983- author. | Aitken, Martin, translator.
Title: The skin is the elastic covering that encases the entire body / Bjørn
Rasmussen; translated from the Danish by Martin Aitken.
Other titles: Huden er det elastiske hylster der omgiver hele legemet. English
Description: San Francisco, CA : Two Lines Press, 2019
Identifiers: LCCN 2018039771 | ISBN 9781931883856 (pbk.)
Classification: LCC PT8177.28.A853 H8313 2019 | DDC 839.813/8--dc23
LC record available at https://lccn.loc.gov/2018039771

1 3 5 7 9 10 8 6 4 2

This book was published with the support of the Danish
Arts Foundation.

**DANISH ARTS FOUNDATION**

# THE SKIN
# IS THE ELASTIC
# COVERING
# THAT ENCASES
# THE ENTIRE
# BODY

# LOVERMAN

I was already older when a man came up to me one day in the lobby of a public place. I saw your play, he said, it touched me more than I can say. I didn't recognize him, but I saw the way he moved, the swagger you get with a certain upbringing in the sticks—he could have been anyone. Do you still smoke, he asked, the heat in here is oppressive, so many people, let's go outside, can I offer you a cigarette.

Very early in my life it was too late. When I got to seventeen it was too late. When I was twelve I filled a sock with semen, all I dreamed about was looking up a man's asshole and breathing that special kind of air, I thought love, a fluttering bird. When I was fifteen and a half the riding instructor appeared.

I think of this picture often, I still see it in my mind, though I've never talked about it. The leather of the breeches on the insides of his thighs, the stitching at the crotch, around the seat, hide against skin. The acrid smell of horse piss, how the ammonia turns the straw red and makes it heavy, the saddle soap, his coarse hands. Yes.

This I know: I groomed the mare; I ate in a cold kitchen with the Brothers, the Mother; her jaw— clack clack. This is the only thing that ties me to the Mother: that dispassionate cheerlessness and clack clack, I can't think of anything else, maybe her fat *because*. This is the Mother's fat *because*:

She woke up one morning and her Loved One wasn't beside her anymore. Can he have gone to the sea, she wondered, can he have gone to the grocery for figs and artichokes, can he be out in the stables. When night came the Mother searched the ditches of the darkland. She imagined her Loved One bleeding, mauled by wolves, and like a wolf she howled at the sky, she wailed and screamed in the night's frost. When day came she wrapped herself in purple and carried great metal buckets of cement to the ditches where she'd been, and filled the ditches up as if to cross them out and say: he wasn't here.

Let me say this: I'm fifteen and a half years old.

I'm on the bus, the 491 to Fjaltring.

I haven't gotten changed, I'm meant to come like this, reeking of horse; it says so in the contract, here's the instruction: take your clothes off, you stink of shit. The sun coming in through the bus window; the flat fields, the sea. It's the first time I've gone to see him.

I live at a state-run boarding school. I eat, sleep, study; I'm seventeen years old, this I know. I know the Mother's got connections or else I wouldn't be here, there are ways of going about things in the sticks, a precedent for preparing *medister* sausages. I know I was sent off on a ferry, the Brothers waved from the dock, the Mother wept, the first goodbye to the Loved One, then the Weimaraner, now the Little One too. I didn't weep. I'd not wept since I fell off a swing at school, the asphalt gouging my knee, but what had occupied me most was the little scrape on the palm of my hand, it was that little drop of blood on the pad of my thumb that made me yell.

The Brothers stared at the knee and were fascinated, the Mother fetched iodine.

The family is concrete, the family is unintentionally blind. This we know. The family exists to remind the Little One that there's such a thing as roots, and roots hurt, roots have to be looked after, this is an obligation, and the location of the roots has to be looked after too, the flag has to be hoisted. These days I dream of flags burning in the streets, I want more respect for textiles than decorating them with symbols and shit, I oppose the adornment of newborns: here's your gender, your name, your flag, your family, may you do your utmost to get rid of it, may you choke on your vomit, may you be sent away.

No, he didn't weep on the deck, that Little One, he's never wept over that family, he's not thrown up since the riding instructor's gin and gin, since he took the riding instructor all the way to the hilt under gin and gin, the Little One's not thrown up, not thrown himself at another since gin and gin, he hasn't breathed that special air he calls love, not since gin and gin, he breathes his air through a vent in the city now, hangs out for tricks and thrusts his hips in provincial parking lots, he's smiling now, and sailing away, and now he's gone.

I've often been told it was the very strong sun of my childhood. My travels abroad each summer with the Brothers, we wouldn't come home until September, long after school had started. The chemistry teacher puts a heavy hand on my shoulder and presses his fat belly against my back, and my dick throbs in my tiny shorts. I've got to stay in my seat for several minutes after the bell rings. My balls are sweaty; my sandals are moist; my feet keep slipping. I try and walk down the corridor properly with piles of paper in my sticky hands, I carry potatoes, stew, and dressed salad from the glass displays in the cafeteria to an empty table, I try and find one that's empty, try and sit down opposite a human being, try and look a human being in the eye, try and find someone I don't want to either fuck or kill. I've often been told it was in my eyes that there was something wrong, that I'd spent too long looking up at the sun, that I was hard to make contact with when I was like that—what was I thinking about, wasn't there something funny about my mouth. The Brothers constantly bared their teeth, they tore apart their cutlets, chewed their exercise books, they laughed.

Let me return to the Mother. One night she went into the Loved One's room and found his trombone. She took it apart, collected the spit and condensation in a little cup. She pulled long tufts of hair from her scalp, soaked them in the cup, and spun eleven slender hounds from them; silver-gray and sleek. These hounds followed her everywhere she went, a train of attendants anyone could see from afar. She in the middle, with her chorus of hounds around her, an oval, effervescent apparition, raw pads against the asphalt, lithe and supple joints, claws. Silver-gray coats glinted in the sun, and the slobber of the hounds rising into the air like soap bubbles.

My life story doesn't exist. I know this now. I used to tell myself it was there somewhere, vibrating, my very own story, that I could somehow get close to it in writing. I was wrong. Never trust a life story. Never trust a man who doesn't want to lick the dick of a man seated on a chair, never trust a man who doesn't want to lick the ass of a woman seated on a chair, never trust a woman who doesn't want to lick the pussy of a woman seated on a chair, never trust a woman who doesn't want to lick the ass of a man seated on a chair, never trust a dick seated on a chair never a pussy seated on a chair on an ass.

I'm saying it the way it sounds.

Write with your asshole, this is a piece of advice to a friend.

I started writing the day the vet came to inseminate the mare. She put a long rubber glove on her hand and excavated great handfuls of shit. Then she injected the stallion's semen into the mare with a thin transparent tube. I was confused by these actions, by shit and semen and ovaries being together, the two holes in the same place—I couldn't work it out; it had me on the brink of tears. I wanted to do a drawing that would help me understand, only I couldn't, my hands were shaking.

I see now that when I was very young, thirteen or fourteen years old, my face was a herald of what alcohol has done to me since. The blobby nose, the skin around the cheekbones, the glassy eyes. I desired everything that could stream through me, my face was an open invitation for wine to ferment in my pores. This perforated face was remarked upon even before I had tasted beer, something stood out and made me different; they called it precociousness, the riding instructor whispered *guilty* one time after a lesson.

I slashed his Kieffer saddle one night.

It happens like this: I sneak a pair of scissors out of the drawer and cross the yard to the stable; I leave the lights off and go through into the tack room, fumbling my way in the dark. I heave air into my lungs, thrust the scissors into the leather, slash the saddle open, and squirt in my riding pants; thrusting, slashing, squirting.

Fifteen and a half.

I get off the bus.

Frost and bright sun, the Mother's worried the water pipes are going to freeze and she'll have to bring buckets to the thirsty animals. I'm worried he's going to send me home on the last bus—there are only three on Saturdays. I can hear the sea from here, I know he swims in winter, I know his nipples shrink and go hard when he swims in winter, that his balls tighten and his dick goes small and juts outward, that the foreskin protects the head. I'm early, I go into the convenience store, they've got cheese and wine, the owners are lesbians—this people know—they don't care if you stink of the stables. You'd better bring something, can't come empty-handed, buy him a bottle of wine, buy him cheese as well, it's what you do, what you

It was during this journey that the picture seemed to separate, it could almost have torn itself from the big picture. If it hadn't been for *because, because*. The

Mother's *because*, the sticks's, the riding instructor's. I say journey because the bus, because Fjaltring, the sea, him. I feel nothing for the big picture, I don't know the big picture, I say city and see nothing, I say the Mother and the Brothers on the farm, I can't take the big picture on, I barely even know the little picture, as such it couldn't have been much of a separation, more likely just a puddle of mud. Sand, grit, clay, what, crust, collapsing soil. When I was ten, God asked me to make all of my moments hold hands. I've never cared much for prayers, I've never cared much for God. Instructions, on the other hand, definitely.

Seventeen and a half.

I get off the bus.

I find the stairs from the car deck and go up through the ferry, out to the railing. The principal stands next to me. Her mouth is pale, her hands slender, she points into the landscape, on her fingers are heavy rings, jade and gold. My journal entries refer to her as the Mistress, the Lady, Madame. I seldom write about the landscape. It runs together like ink blotches, there's no perspective in what I write.

I always get off the bus when we board the ferry, even at night, because I'm always scared, I'm scared the ropes are going to snap, scared we'll drift out to sea. I stand at the railing and look out into the darkness. I'm interested in death by drowning. I'm interested in all sorts of ways of dying, but there's something about drowning I find especially meticulous; the slowness of it, the water's silent intrusion. Yes.

I'm wearing a dress of natural silk. It's tired, nearly see-through. It belongs to the Mother. I've got the place to myself, the Mother's out shooting with her favorite Weimaraner, the Brothers are with her in their brand-new oilskin coats, three sizes too big, laughable twin green tents, in silent awe of the hunters, the instinct of the dogs, the reek of gunpowder and dead game. The Weimaraner's the champ, it wins everything always, the Mother calls it her gray ghost. She's the only woman among them, men are just bastards.

I go from floor to floor, inspecting the place; it's like seeing it for the first time. I pass my fingertips over the cold granite in the kitchen, the pickles and preserves in the pantry, the Argentine porcelain in the display cabinet in the dining room. I move slowly through the rooms, my bare feet writing forth the floor, the wooden floor, step-by-step.

The oriental rugs in the living room, the fireplace's open crater, ashes in my big, new hands.

I crawl inside the fireplace, I can only just stand up in it, bending my back.

I look up into the dark shaft.

They come home with the dead Weimaraner in a blanket. The Brothers are weeping; they busy themselves around the Mother, making her some tea. She leaves the tea untouched, sits there straight, and stares into space. That's when I notice her mouth. A cold shiver runs through me. Her mouth: stupid and cruel. She doesn't look at me when she says: I'm going to kill them. I'm going to kill those bastards.

I'm covered in soot. I've still got the dress on.

It's not the dress that makes the Little One's appearance so noticeable on this particular day, because the Little One isn't wearing the dress now, he's wearing a shirt and jacket, a tie with a tie-pin, white leather riding breeches, white gloves, boots, and spurs. No, it's the hat, a soft pink felt hat. It's the day before the Weimaraner's burial beneath the conifer, and the question is still: Who shot it?

The whole family's there, the stable hand, the riding girls, *he's* there too. The Little One hasn't touched him yet, the contract's not yet in force, not even drawn up, not even imagined possible: you don't shower without my permission, you don't give me gifts or pay me compliments, no flowers or wine, you do as I say.

The Mother is veiled in black, she makes a long speech, her cold voice borne along by the wind blowing in the trees; she quotes Blixen, Brorson; the Brothers serve eggnog in smoke-colored glasses.

The Little One and the mare perform a display of mourning in the big arena, classical music marks the rhythm of the paces. During the canter-work and Mozart, the Mother starts hyperventilating. They try to calm her, press on her chest, press on her back, bring her water, but she only gasps louder for air. The Little One continues his performance: flying changes, half-passes, piaffe. The mare is utterly responsive, precision never better. The Little One has practiced his position and posture with a whip across his back held in the crooks of his elbows, now he has dispensed with the whip and sits completely erect, the mare foams at the mouth and gives up her back to him, they are a team, horse and rider. At the violins' cue, the heralding of the end, they ride up to the seated audience, and on the final note of the trombone they halt. The Little One grips the flat brim of his felt hat and lifts it, and on that final trumpet blast, as he holds the hat out to the side, arm outstretched, the Mother passes out. Everyone's over her, bustling, trembling, wailing. Only the instructor remains facing the horse and rider.

He looks straight into my eyes.
Yes.

I dug out a photo of my son at the age of seventeen. No. I dug out a photo of me at the age of seventeen and thought: That's someone's son. How thin he is. How little he still is. And yet: the face, how guilty it looks, how full of fire. Why? Is he imagining five unborn children, are they baying at his sleeve, does he really think semen is in any way valid? If he still has some notion of happiness, then it's something from a pop song, an affectation; where's that photo from, where's it from?

The person who bought that pink hat with the flat brim and broad black band, this is her, this woman in this particular photograph—she's my mother. It shows her posing on a beach, she's still young, eighteen, perhaps, or twenty. It was on this holiday she bought the hat, it was here she met the Loved One;

this decisive event, has it already occurred here in this photograph, is he the one taking my mother's picture on the beach, or is it a girlfriend, a tourist, one of the locals. She's wearing a yellow bathing suit.

These photographs, there are so many of them. I keep them in a drawer of my desk, they're loose and get mixed up. I don't try and kid myself that the moment they were taken can be held forever, but nor can it be let go of. What are you supposed to do with photographs, what. What are you supposed to do with moments. You can be so gung ho, so hard as nails one day, such a failure the next, staggering around in the ditches, coughing up bits of blood, yes.

And you don't even recognize your Loverman in the lobby of a public place.

Only when I go outside and smoke with him. Only when I flick the lighter in front of his cigarette, which he holds between thumb and index finger, only when he puts his hand around my wrist to catch the flame with the cigarette's end. Only then does the realization rattle through me. Only then does the picture appear. Or the sounds, maybe I should call it the sounds.

sound, and a stabbing, burning sensation emanated from my pupils. After a while I thought my eyes were going to burst. When I eventually fell asleep, I dreamed: I get up, take Mom's car, and drive out to Fjaltring. I can hardly see through the windshield, the night's crisp and clear with frost, but my eyes. The frequencies of the car radio merge with my teeming thoughts, and I realize there's no difference. I'm an open shell, amenable to whatever. I'm the potholes in the gravel road, the hole for the gasoline in the car; I keep getting filled; it's a momentous discovery.

For a little while tonight I was totally calm inside. I groomed Magna, picked her hooves, picked her tail, picked the dirt from between her teats; she's very pregnant now and they're swollen. I still ride her, we practice some dressage, only half an hour, but concentrated. I often think of the horses as a tragic Greek chorus, I think of them singing. It's being touched by humans that makes them sing. The more we run our fingers through their manes and tails, rub grease into their hooves, the more we warm the bit in our hands before putting it in their mouths. In the woods with him at Christmas they sang. Bright sun. He held my hand. He'd never held my hand before, the contract says nothing about holding hands, nothing about: kissing, caressing. I put my arms around a big tree and he tied my hands with that blue cord they use to keep hay bales together. He left me like that for quite some time, hugging the tree, nose and lips pressed against the rough bark. I don't know where he was, maybe he went back to the car, maybe he sat down on a tree stump and watched me, smoked a cigarette. I heard only the faint song of the horses; the sun on my exposed neck.

Upstairs in the sterile, white bathroom that smelled of warm skin and toothpaste, I leaned over the sink in my thoughtless ritual, cleaned the sore and the other places as prescribed, and admired the gleaming chrome, the cool light dazzling about the taps. Believe nothing of what I say about feelings. My desire is an adjustment to the central heating system, I am stage scenery comprised of human organs. Tell me about atoms, tell me about implosion. The lungs, they oxygenate the blood, this we know. The liver, red-brown and cone-shaped, weighing a kilogram and a half. The kidneys, the stomach, the intestines: the small intestine, the duodenum. I can do without the large intestine, all I need is a bag on my belly to collect the fluids; I'm just a bagful of bacteria myself, nothing more. The spleen too I can do without, and one lung, one kidney, and 4/5 of the red-brown liver, most of it's sugar and fat deposits, we know this.

Your letter just came, the one about your walk along the sea, about war. About you wanting to break the contract. I'm reading that between the lines. Am I right? If so, I'd ask you to tell me straight, I'd ask you not to write stuff between the lines, do you think I'm stupid or something?

I got so scared reading that fucking letter that I bit down so hard on my tongue it started to bleed. As far as I understand it, you can't just walk out on a contract. You'd better believe me: I'm going to let all this out of the bag if you break it off; I'll go straight to Mom and tell her what you've done. She knows people, you know that, and I've got marks all over my body, who's to say they're not from you; I can make a case, no problem, I can tell them you're dangerous. I wouldn't even have to do that, all it takes is a bit of graffiti on a bus shelter, in the bathrooms at school—*pedo scum*—no one survives a rumor like that around here; you do realize that, don't you.

I mean it. I'll cut the dick off your fucking stupid gelding, I will. I'll put laxatives in his feed, I'll do it tomorrow, and if you ignore me again during our next lesson, I'll smear his salt lick with glue. As for the war, was that a hypocrite I heard, shitting his load on the paper; was it the height of masculine delusion I sensed there; between the lines did I read a dream of gunfire and the chilly hand of God on your brow on a hot June day? If you really intend to take part in that war, I'm not going to be the one to stop you. Sign up and get yourself down there, fill your lungs and scream for the mother cunt-ry, kill some Arabs, those are my instructions.

OK then, say hello to God from me, tell him he's a bastard. Say hello to your Nazi heart, say hello to your dick.

Yours sincerely, Bjørn.


I'm sitting here in a deep, upholstered armchair with grasshoppers chirping, creaking, wanking away outside. I've got no clothes on. It's like the chair's yellow upholstery is seeping half a centimeter into my skin and spreading a warm light inside me, it's like the grasshoppers are programmed to get me going. I'm tranquility itself. Suddenly there's no resistance.

I just let myself out of his loft. I've been sat there five hours, six hours, hands cuffed behind my back, the key at the bottom of a big bucket of frozen water. It was hot in there, the radiator on high, but a bucket of ice like that takes ages to melt. The first hour, I must have checked with my toes ten, twenty times, the second hour I started to panic. He went away as soon as he snapped the cuffs on, he drove home to Mom, she's got the spring event going on, I can't ride Magna, she's too swollen. You can start on Castro, she said, you can ride an LB2 on Don Juan. I said no. I'm going on a weekend trip with Dad, I said, looking her in the eye. She did that thing with her mouth. I've never brought it on before, never said no to her, never spoken the word *dad*, it doesn't exist.

Anyway, there I am, shut inside his loft while he's off judging. In my perspiring, palpitating ecstasy I picture him seated in the judge's box, observing the riders and horses, dishing out points for paces, impulsion, submission, position, and seat: 6/12, 7/14. He speaks his comments aloud, the Brothers take turns being the scribe, obediently writing down every word that comes out of his mouth, his fleshy lips: wrong canter, more forward, good walk, well ridden, precise. His teeth and tongue spitting his dark voice into my ear—hammer, anvil, stirrup—the precise punch of his bass in my nerve paths, it typewrites my heart to a canter, it impels my blood, and I am turned into quivering, soft texture, and sound.

I am wildly in love with you. But I can't come to your lessons for a while. Magna has miscarried, she needs time to grieve, and I won't ride another. And I think I'm splitting apart. Whenever I see you. Having to pretend there's nothing between us. It's the same old story. I shake uncontrollably just seeing your car on the gravel out front.

In time I suppose I'll get used to the idea of a man and kids, that it's never going to be. In time I suppose I'll stop thinking about it. In time I'll be able to get the train to Lemvig without thinking about anything at all. Have I mentioned Lemvig? Lemvig is Happyville, West Jutland. Lemvig is built on a bed of boiled medister sausage, this is fact. The street grid in Lemvig is structured on the principle of *sylte*. Sylte is made from the meat of a pig's head, especially the cheek. The church in Lemvig is the shank, the harbor the stock, rich with gelatin; the sweet ale is the pig's blood, and the cafeteria's curry ketchup is the residue from the bowel.

How intricate and complex a mechanism the nervous system is! The telephone's electric shrillness sends a tremor of excitement through the perineum; the sound of his abrasive, brash, confidential voice on the line prompts the intestines to contract.

Yesterday when I got off the bus, I went into the convenience store and bought a bottle of wine. The checkout woman, the busty one, picked a piece of straw out of my hair and gave me a wink.

When I got through the door and handed him the wine, he ordered me into the bathtub. He sat on the toilet seat taking swigs from the bottle as the scalding water rose around my body. When the bathtub was half filled he poured the rest of the wine over the head of my dick, which stuck up above the surface. Then he unbuttoned his trousers, got his own big brown cock out, and pissed all over my chest, in my hair, my mouth.

I came. I screamed. I love him.

Eddie, I thought. Sometimes I'm glad you're my brother. You just knocked on the door of my room because you wanted to show me something. I went with you into the stable and up into the hay loft. There was the placenta, Magna's placenta from the foal she miscarried. You'd been told to give it to the dogs after the unhappy event, they love to slobber over the afterbirth, and Mom reckons they can stomach it, but you hid it instead, because you wanted to comfort your little brother. It's already started to rot, but you emptied your deodorant on it to lessen the stench and keep the flies away. I've promised not to tell Vilhelm. I didn't think you had secrets from each other. I didn't think you were individually minded, had different wants and needs like that. I've got so many wants and needs that

I'm ugly tonight. Someone should put a bolt through my head, like they do with pigs, and horses too. No one will ever feel happy with me. I'm too stupid to meet interesting people, I've got too many fresh wounds to put a T-shirt on and be sexy and unselfconscious; the skin is a stage, as everyone knows. The skin is a stage where people express their inner worlds, the skin is the elastic covering that encases the entire body, the skin covers a surface area of between 1.6 and 1.8 square meters, the equivalent of a regular duvet cover. The skin is thinner in children and women than in men, the skin is thinner in older people than in young people, the thinnest skin, located on the eyelids and genitals, is 0.5 mm thick, the skin of young people like me is yellow-white with a blush of red, and when we're old it's gray-white with a blush of blue, its color varies according to the amount of blood and fat in the subcutis. The skin has a characteristically matte sheen resembling silk or satin, due to the refraction of light from the many fine irregularities on its surface. If this surface texture becomes flattened by the skin being stretched, as in the case of pregnancy, a cyst, or other such growth, the skin will become shiny and reflective. The skin reflects our feelings toward the world. It blushes, pales, perspires. We tan our skins, we use cosmetics.

Now I think I know what loneliness is. I slashed his Kieffer saddle last night. He used it this afternoon. He went past me in the aisle of the stable, glanced at me in passing, and smiled a friendly, overbearing smile. I went out to the Rom Riding Club— he instructs there on Tuesday nights. I went to the cafeteria, bought myself some fries and a box of synthetic raspberry juice, sat down on a big round silage bale, and watched the lesson. He strode around in the middle of the arena, instructing the riders with his usual confidence, the measured bass of his voice, the firm gestures. When he ordered the riders into a walk, I pissed myself slightly. When he left the arena I died.

Now we sit around the corpse. Now the corpse is considered, now the corpse is presented on a bed of sushi. Now the corpse becomes the site of a delicate incision indeed, a finely cut pachisi board. Allow the use of the pronoun *I* in reference to this corpse. Allow this *I* to apply for the job of pachisi board: Hi. I'm not a cheerful young man with plenty of get-up-and-go and tanned legs in summer. I'm not the romantic type inclined to candlelit dinners and relaxing with red wine on the sofa, I'm not a single who loves a fun night out with a friend, I don't go up to the DJ and implore, *Play my song, please, impeach my bush.* I'm not the sort who sings in the shower, I don't have a good pop song on the brain, *I would have given you all of my heart,* for example. *But there's someone who has torn it apart,* for example. *And he's taking almost all that I've got,* for example. I don't have those phrases down pat, my mind's like a sieve, a sow, a sea, sadness, security. I don't have that little bit of homeland tucked between the ribs, I've got no feelings for the flag, for history, language, or art, the sex organs, the body. I've got fuck all consideration under my larynx, I don't look at myself in the mirror and say, I love you, I love you, I love you, I love you. That's not me at all. My shaved balls aren't mine, nor are my inner labia. My long trumpet dick, the thick bush around my clit isn't mine. And the slender waist, the narrow hips, the narrow literature I intend to write in a hut in the woods with the slime trails of snails traced on my inner thighs, ticks burrowed into my groin, acne across my shoulders, the pizza of skin on my back, this neither. I haven't quit milk and wheat flour, and so you could go on—there's always something you can quit. And I will, soon. So there's no need for you to reply, you'd be wasting your time and mine; so there, I've said it, it's not my gorgeous body you see in the album, I cut and pasted it off the internet, but there you go. My face. My awful face. Mine. The red threads in the whites of my eyes, and my nose, that blobby vacuum cleaner, and my mouth, my unflagging asshole, the ass of my face, I'm trying to do something about it. Or maybe not trying, I don't know, I know fuck all, my life is fuck all, I don't want you to contact me. Try trying, if things are that trying. Try breathing exercises and tea, try keeping it in, try holding your hand, try cutting the skin along the grain, the healing's quicker, the scars are finer. *And there's nobody home. The building is empty and there's nobody home. And in the next house and in the next house and in the next house there's nobody home.* For example.

# LITTLE BJØRN

I think Bjørn availed himself of the wild migrating birds in order to slip away. On the morning he left, he went into the stable. The sickly warm stench assailed him as soon as he stepped inside. It was the horses. They had begun to decompose. They stood quite still but were coming apart. A large hunk of meat came away from a shoulder blade and fell into the stiff, yellow straw. A lengthy slit in a groin split open and the entire hindquarters collapsed: haunches, tail, spine crumbling away like grain. An eye plopped from its socket and hung from slimy fibers, dangled a moment at the weeping muzzle until the final filament separated and the eye fell to the ground. The revolting sight overran him, he gasped for breath, he ran from the stable and vomited in the cold snow. There too they stood. The horses. They were all around, frozen to death, frigid statues with lips pulled back, teeth exposed. But one horse was still breathing. It was the mare.

The faintest steam came from her nostrils. She creaked as she turned her head to look at him. A tiny, ice-cold snap of the neck. A shudder of the orbs. Glassy, knife-like pupils in black.

Farewell, said the Little One. But the mare did not reply.

Farewell, he said again. The mare did not reply. But it looked at him.

I've been silly, he said, and held his palm out toward her muzzle. Please forgive me.

The mare put her tongue out between her bared, tawny teeth and licked the Little One's hand twice, three times. I love you, she said. Try to be happy.

I'm not sure, the Little One trembled. I don't think I can.

Don't stand there wasting time, the mare cut in. You've already decided. Go now.

For she did not wish to see him cry.

So he went.

# BJØRN IS A DREAM

When Bjørn came to the realization that a person needs meaningful employment in order to survive in this world, he found the address of a brothel in the city's Vesterbro quarter and staggered to it. A girl of the night received him, her mouth painted red, black hair in a bob cut.

The poor knight returns, she announced, as if they had known each other for a long time.

Let me give you a bubble bath, make you feel at home.

The girl tied a white blindfold around the poor knight's eyes so that the night would fall gently. He resisted at first, lashing out with fists and feet, biting into her small, pale breasts; but eventually he succumbed, the sounds in his eyes became quiet, he grew calm.

You've fallen afoul of the times, read: the rigors of the age, the girl said, capitalism. We all have to go through it. My body's been an unreported brothel ever since I saw my first Disney movie, ever since I recited my first Lord's Prayer in school. This profession simply takes the bull by the horns; now it's the bull licking *my* business—read: cunt— instead of the other way around.

The girl covered Bjørn's scarred frame with sheets of saddle leather before going on: My cunt is a turkey, they like that around here, they like when it gobbles. The goal is to get it to shut the fuck up, and goals make them horny. I'm no silent whore, I find speaking erotic—language gives me the biggest orgasms.

The Mistress who entered that miserable loft was scrawny, hunchbacked, and missing an eye.

Who's this? she hissed on seeing the person so enshrouded.

The knight, the whore replied. He wishes to join us, Madame.

The Mistress pinched the knight's cheek. She tapped her heavy rings, jade and gold, against the bridge of his nose twice, three times.

He's too thin, she spat. Take a cast.

Of his dick?

Of everything, the Mistress cried. All of it!

Skin and bone!

Why?

To assess the demand. When it's done, I'll decide.

But I've got a client, the girl stammered.

The client can wait.

But the turkey, she persisted, the money.

There's plaster of Paris in the cupboard, you know where the gauze is.

As the Mistress contemplated the blue-black and purple pattern on Bjørn's body, which she couldn't see now because of the plaster, the whore explained: He's been made sick by homosexual love. He says he killed his horse, a bolt through its head. He keeps raving about Jesus Christ and the nature of war. He says he's ready, set, raring to be an adult, read: to abandon his youthful reveries of ambitious activism in the struggle against capitalist conceptions of happiness and contentment. The competent individual, the individual with purchasing power. The purchased individual: The infected, IKEA-lized, fabricated, laminated individual. The gendered, gentrified, bright-eyed, rosy-cheeked individual. The counselorized, bastardized, groomed and galvanized, tanned and toothpasted individual.

Flawless, impeccable, consummate, complete, and totally individualized: individual. It's the same old story. He turned up with a liter and a half of gin and twenty-seven raspberry tarts in a paper bag, nothing else.

Bjørn, now encased in plaster of Paris, was unable to speak. Nor even see. But he could hear, and although he barely understood what was being said, the sound of the Mistress's crackling voice mingling with the brighter tone of the whore's made him feel good.

Give him five tricks and a decent meal, then we'll see.

Fillet of veal? Smoked venison?

Soup! Chili with chicken!

Can he try women? My turkey wants to train him.

No. The Mistress smoothed the girl's cheek, tucked a black strand behind her right ear, the pierced, more protruding one, and said: Men. He needs to be cured.

Cured? the girl repeated, and raised her plucked eyebrows.

Cured of love, bitch. Love in general. Look at him! Now shut your turkey!

Bjørn signs his second ever contract. He places fat little crosses next to all twenty-seven of the itemized sexual preferences. The Mistress is visibly impressed. She finds him a studio in Nordvest, and soon the tricks are lined up at his sheets.

Bjørn is a cocksucking dream; Bjørn can guzzle a 22 cm dick to the hilt while simultaneously using his tongue on the taut testicles—like a cat licking the grease from a pair of freshly hatched pigeons—Bjørn's mouth is a warm and greedy grotto, Bjørn swallows sperm like milk and honey.

Bjørn's dick is the most pliable granite to neglected assholes, Bjørn's balls slap against smoothly shaved buttocks for hours on end, Bjørn takes his whip to inner thighs, lashes backs until they bleed, ties hands and feet, fastens clamps to sacks, perinea, and nipples. Bjørn is an Arab stallion, squirting warm, white semen against blood-red palates, the sickly whiff of shit wafting from the dick-collar.

Bjørn rides two men at once, his anus insatiable and untiring. Bjørn's boy-cunt is an elastic sheath that could snap a pinkie off at the root just before consuming a hairy laborer's fist and forearm without splitting even a millimeter.

Yes.

When Bjørn received his first paycheck at the end of the month, his wounds were healed, the fatiguing sound in his eyes was gone, and he had put on considerable mass thanks to the gym next door to the brothel. His mind had erased the Mother and the Brothers, the horses and hounds, he remembered absolutely nothing of the rigors he had gone through on his journey toward this, his adult life. He performed his good deeds for the day and earned himself a shitload of dough. Indeed, one might be tempted to suggest that he was now happy, were it not for this novel, growing feeling that had implanted itself in the depths of his brain: he had begun to think of wealth as a thing of beauty, and was becoming insanely infatuated with it. He began to personify wealth the way religious people personify God:

I wish by bloody Christ that this love between us didn't keep me captive like a lunatic. I know you're omnipotent, I feel your strong, sweet breath in my pores wherever I go, but you come on so transactional, so virtual and abstract, and I realize you won't bind yourself to time and place, but why not? I'm asking you now, will you manifest yourself to me? You've taken over my body, you see, you've monopolized my thoughts and feelings. I'm your business, I'm your whore, only I'm unreported, can't you come and report me, seriously? Can't you at least send a backup in your place, can't you send your rugby mates, can't they bring their bats with them, I mean your baseball buddies, I mean that Brian Mikkelsen from the government. I'm asking you—can't we be a bit concrete here—can't Brian Mikkelsen come and mutilate my foreskin with paper flags, can't Brian Mikkelsen come and give me a code word, an amorous command, can't Brian Mikkelsen come and hiss *Blåvandshuk* in my ear before giving me the kiss of death, thereby depriving me of these dregs of depleting self-awareness, then squeeze his yellowy semen out onto my deceased and chivalrous belly, oh yes, can't you commit murder on me tonight, can't you lay me down on a bed of avocados, stoned and overripe, are they from Kvickly or the Arab grocery store—I'm so overwrought, I can sleep 24/7—or maybe from the 7-Eleven, I'm begging you, just fuck me harder, like really thrust, wipe me out completely, or turn me up, turn me right up until I can't hear anything else, just give me a system for Christ's sake, for example: Carve a cross into your chest, a centimeter and a half, and for every bacteria-infested pigeon I chase out of this studio carve another going the other way, thereby forming a pattern of checks, then lie down in a heavenly bed, lie there totally shriveled and happy, and play tic-tac-toe on your own chest with your grandchildren straddling your belly. Just eat cauliflower and remember to shit and be totally *gone* inside, be a doll and nothing else, a doll everyone wants to play with: skin on skin every time someone moves a piece.

Bjørn has a dream about love between human beings. The lovers manifest themselves as chickens with their heads chopped off. The bodies flap around blindly in the gravel, bumping into each other at random. The turmoil of feathers, the pumping spurts of blood from the arteries. Bjørn tosses the heads into the dog pen and the silver-gray ghosts descend on them. Bjørn dips the headless lovers in barrels of boiling water and plucks off their plumage. He caresses their knobbly skin, one after the other, and makes a fine long incision from throat to rectum. He removes the gizzard, the guts, the liver. He holds out the lovers' hearts in the dusty light that streams in through the window of the utility room. On the shelves are ancient jars of preserved ginger, gooseberries, redcurrants. Bjørn stuffs the dead chickens, he prepares an exquisite romantic dinner—you have to be a vegetable to love, this we know, the body has to be programmed for dreams. And indeed there are vegetables on the table, there are parsnips, beets, even celery, creamed artichoke hearts, naturally, and date butter, dewy grapes, the chickens themselves: crisp and bulging on their silver plate, their glazed, fried hearts topped with curled parsley, lemon: this is seduction, this is the prelude to penetration, a feasibility of fatal fertilization, stop it before it's too late, make sure always to support abortion rights, chop the head off that poor embryo, give it the ecstasy of gravel, give it feathers and the fewest of seconds, before the end.

Bjørn had another dream, about a handsome man in leather riding boots, sharply pointed spurs, and a heavy titanium piercing through the head of his dick. This man could make gin into helium. Bjørn inhaled fiercely and made keen use of his tiny new voice. His feet left the ground, he floated. The more sentences his tiny voice formed, the higher he flew, fastened by the thinnest of silver threads to the handsome man's intimate piercing.

I'm saying it the way it is, the way it sounds. Can Bjørn come to terms with having an indefinite mind in a definite body? Can Bjørn find a way to live, read: love? I don't know. I know the Egyptians described their experiences with the treatment of wounds in the year 1500 BC. They placed long strips on the wound, smeared with resin, oils, and honey. A thousand years later the Indians used cotton, ash, and butter. A hundred years later came Hippocrates, the father of medicine; he used wine, vinegar, boiled water; I know this. I know that the rectum of the mare should not be examined between the thirtieth and the thirty-ninth day after covering, since in this period some rather complex hormonal cell migrations occur in the mare's uterus. I know the most reliable way of telling if a mare is in heat is to bring her to a stallion and observe for the usual signs: she will elevate her tail, scrape her hind legs, and wink her vulva, which will be red and swollen and expel a transparent slime.

Let me return to the exquisite romantic dinner. For who was sitting there at the table but Bjørn and the handsome man; they had scarfed down everything. And who was the handsome man but the riding instructor, the Loverman himself! And what did the Loverman do? He got to his feet and grabbed Bjørn by the collar and hauled him onto the dining table and got on top of him with all of his ninety-nine kilograms and said: Now you're going to rim me one last time. After this you won't see me for a year. You won't contact me in any way, and you're not to be intimate with anyone else, you're forbidden to have sex for a year. We need to stabilize the way you perceive yourself, do you understand what I'm saying?

I place my small hands, my big hands, against the riding instructor's firm, brown, round buttocks with their fair covering of down, and spread them. I bury my nose in the crack, fix my lips to the tight flesh, pink and gray, and proceed to suck and slobber and lick. My tongue penetrates the ring of his anus, caresses the inner walls.

I look up into the dark shaft.

And the horses sing.


Now that Bjørn wasn't allowed to have sex for a year, which is as good as forever, he no longer knew if there was anything to live for. He knocked on the door of the Mistress's private rooms and said: Your mission has been a success. I'm no longer capable of love. Men are bastards. The Mistress stood there gaping, but Bjørn continued: I want to restructure the contract, I want to spend the rest of my life drinking myself to death. I want to give up my back as a real-life and virtual game board. I'm willing to incorporate electrodes into my body, I'm willing to video record the breakdown of my organs with tiny endoscopic cameras, I'm willing to blog.

The Mistress smoothed Bjørn's cheek, her pale mouth smiling, and said: You've got an orgy in fifteen minutes, go and shower.

I don't fuck anymore, he insisted. Accept my backboard offer.

The Mistress looked at him. Then told him to pack his things.

Bjørn was down on his knees and peering through a keyhole, and his eye met that of the girl—red mouth and black hair, fanny fuck-full of fist.

Farewell?

Farewell.


Love between human beings only occurs when a person is suffering for absolutely no reason. Bjørn wrote this on his computer. He had bought a computer from the Fona electronics store, and a suit of armor from a costume sale at the Royal Danish Theatre, and he had rented an apartment on the street called Gartnergade in Copenhagen.

In the mornings, he put on the armor and propelled himself slowly and with much creaking from the living room to the kitchen to the bathroom, and then back again. He drank gin and gin. He came by his own hand. He kept indoors— Copenhagen long since definitively mapped—and there was no way he could cycle in such an outfit anyway. From his desk by the window he observed the gangly, acrobatic skipping of Arab girls, their theatrical posing between the swinging ropes: Your mo-om. Your mo-om. Your mo-om. The rhythm of their rhymes ran through him at night, his nightmares were monotonous: the Mother's ice-cold bedroom, the screams, her saggy boobs at the beach, the thick bush surrounding her clit. The dogs knocked him down at the water's edge, their sharp claws, their long wet tongues, slobber and salt in the scratches on his skin, the imperceptible encroachment of sand into ears, nose, throat.

His family was willing to take him back and let him be theirs again. The Brothers wrote a letter together about health and girlfriends and wanting him home for Christmas. They arrived at Copenhagen's Central Station with backpacks and wax in their hair. They put their arms around him and he went with them to the Tivoli Gardens; they dined expensively at an Italian, a Mexican, a French restaurant, and drank wine. The Brothers told him their mother had cancer, that she had sold the warmbloods for a song. These were Eddie's words, the latter, he smiled tentatively and reached his hand out across the table to his brother. But Bjørn only looked at them both and said: I'm not going anywhere. I've made up my mind.

The Brothers started to laugh, thinking he was putting them on; we've missed you, said Vilhelm, come back with us, come home. Bjørn looked at them, smiled, and said: Try and be happy.

The Brothers started to cry, their feelings were too much for them. Eddie made a scene, threw his wine in Bjørn's face, hugged and squeezed him, begged. Vilhelm wanted to go. And so they went.

## YOU MY YOU

I'm writing this to give you an idea about what I'm like. Having to be someone can be rather a depleting form of conceit. It's an immensely tiresome project, trying to rid oneself of everything one is *not*, as in: attach vacuum to solar plexus, locate and perform removal of foreign bodies in own body, be with you in a sec. But you asked for it, it was your instruction, so obviously I'll do as I'm told, lap it up, of course I will, *the first cut is the deepest*, and I'm already older, twenty-four, twenty-five, when one day you come up to me in the lobby of a public place. I recognize you right away. The blood rushes through me.

You gave me a lift from the Rom Riding Club back to the farm. We didn't say a word in the car. Not until you pulled up in front of the stable, turned off the engine, and said: Bjørn, I'm not coming anymore. I'm moving Frühling this weekend and won't be coming anymore.

I said it the way it was: I love you.

I'm sorry, Bjørn, I really am, but I can't go on with this.

I love you.

Cut it out.

I love you.

Cut it out, now.

You were right behind me as I turned the corner of the barn. You screamed my name after me, a lunge whip in your hand, and I ran as fast as I could. He's going to kill me, I thought. He's going to kill me now. When I got to the stable door, my mother stepped out in front of me. She held the tail up in the air, her arm fully extended.

Did you do this?

The image of that. The rage in my mother's face, her dreadful, trembling mouth, the straw stuck to the green at the throat of her sweater. And her clenched, chalk-white hand around the gelding's long, thick tail—a profusion of glistening black hair. I quivered in fear, I sobbed and gasped for air, I wanted to turn and face you, but I was too scared. My spine was on fire. Waiting for the lash of the whip.

After I've gone outside to smoke with you, after I've held the lighter in front of your cigarette, which you hold between thumb and index finger, after you've put your hand around my wrist to catch the flame with the end of your cigarette, you tell me you live in the woods near Sabro. There's a tree there that weeps, it's got this bulge across the trunk, like a mouth with a harelip, and a hole a bit further up, like an eye, and this eye weeps resin, thick, glistening resin that trickles down the trunk.

Let's go, I say.

I was just about to whisper to you and suggest we find another shop when the keeper of the gold put the perfect ring on my furious finger and placed my hand next to yours on the counter; yours that had already been wearing exactly the right-sized ring for some time.

And so we walked in the woods, ringed and rattling with desire, and you had your homemade knapsack of ash-white canvas and birch across your shoulder: bread, gin, aquavit, two grams of skunk weed. I tried to climb the weeping tree and scratched my inner thigh, making it bleed; my small white shorts were smeared green by the bark, streaked with brown-red blood. You poured gin on the scrape from your cupped hand and licked it clean; you tore a yellow strip from your T-shirt and tied it around my thigh with the blue cord that tied the knapsack.

When the weed kicked in, you waded into the pond. I watched you standing there, the red remains of evening winking in the water that surrounded you from the hips down. The pronounced *V* of your Apollo's belt reflected in the surface, ripples caressed your pubic hair, the insects flitted around you.

You were crying. I'd never seen you cry before. You've cried many times since, and with good reason; my two hands aren't enough to count the times you've been pained to the bone, but at the time: your chest heaved, snot ran from your nose, the sound you made was like a stag maimed by a botched rifle shot. You roared.

We don't like seeing our rings vanish into the pond in the woods. I don't know what makes us do it. A feeling.

You stop crying and lie on the bank chewing bread; I take it from you and throw it away. We make love in the reeds. You look me in the eye during the entire act, big black pupils ringed with brown; you spit a mash of soft white bread into my mouth; the hairs on your chest glisten green with algae slime. What's a ring, anyway. What's a reed, what's bread, what's a heart.

She repeated the message plainly in English: Passengers must not leave their baggage unattended at any time.

We were sitting in a stuffed train compartment heading in the direction of Struer, we had duffel bags with us, tote bags and presents in boxes, I felt like leaving all of it behind and getting off somewhere random—Skive, Viborg—only you were insistent on goose and a family reunion, we were going to Lemvig, and like a fat white goose you had the same glassy look in your eye of an excited kid on Christmas Eve, worked up into that pre-orgasmic state, oh the presents, oh the idyll, oh God.

Have I mentioned Lemvig? Have I mentioned God?

Lemvig is Happyville, West Jutland. Lemvig can be separated into *Lem* and *Vig*. If you've got a *lem* in Lemvig, which is a dick, you're obliged by unstated law to fondle the buttocks of any female who happens to pass by in broad daylight in

Lemvig, the more fondling and the more high-lights in your hair, the closer you come to God. If you've got a pair of vulval labia in Lemvig, and the pink flesh of those labia contrast with surrounding black, and those black-skinned buttocks are fondled by someone who happens to pass by with a fair-skinned *lem*, which is a dick, in broad daylight in Lemvig, then you're obliged by unstated law to either *vige* (*Vig!*), which is to yield (Yield!), or spread those buttocks for said *lem*, which is a dick (*Lem!* Dick!). But alas, the more buttocks that are spread, the more *lem*, which is a dick, the further one grows removed from God. This we know.

And yet there we sat stuffed into a train compartment, soon to arrive in Struer, where the Brothers would pick us up in the car. Salute.

In the meantime you kept a tight hold on the presents and I said you were ruining the shape of your jacket by filling your pockets like that: wallet, pocketknife, handkerchief—masculine things I'm pleased you carry around, especially the wallet, an exceedingly intimate object, and totally private, my hands tremble when I rifle through it, it's like it's you, if you could appear in object form, if any object, you'd be it, black leather, worn, with lots of compartments and little hiding places for notes. I read your text messages too, and your emails, and there's a reason my hands are shaking, because this came in yesterday:

You will have free rein. You will assess the prevailing mood at any given time, moving about without restriction within the military hierarchy. Your function will be extended to include taking care of institutional cohesion and morale. You should consider it your natural ambition to make the camp work. Basically, you'll be getting asses in gear. *Operation Bad Ass*. You know?

I brush some fluff off your shoulder, wipe a stain from your lapel, and behave to all intents and purposes like your wife for the duration of the bus ride. You're already a bit dead as you stand there in the airport in your military gear, weighed down by bags. I'm veiled in black, apart from the aubergine headscarf, a silent but typical demonstration on my part, the membrane between us is intact. But my eyes say it the way it is, which is:

I'd happily die in a trench with you at my side.

I'd happily explode in the mud.

Although soup is definitely preferable to porridge or sour milk, it was with visible skepticism you went about the meatballs and dumplings.

I read your letter while doing the dishes, the radio playing quiet, smoochy pop: *Can, can you forgive me, can you cha cha cha my name.* The stuff we were told in Home Ec at school has stuck: glasses first, then the cutlery, then the plates, *can you save me maybe from going insane.* I've hired a clairvoyant to find out if you're going to be coming home again. She says I'm to imagine filling a big egg with light when I'm sitting on the Metro. But there's no Metro in Sabro, only a tree that weeps. She gives me the session on a CD to take home, I transcribe it and send it to you. You write back: Do as she says, go fetal and breathe.

> My hands wrinkle in the soapy water.
> *This is very hard for me.*
> *I don't know what love is.*
> *I don't want to be alone.*

When it's time to die, when we've gotten old, white as the forgotten chocolates in those boxes we've got in our grubby glass-fronted cabinet, presents from some distant birthday, which we occasionally offer

with trembling hands to younger relatives who po-
litely shake their heads and decline, we'll drive off a
cliff and be split into atoms, but not now, not until
2060.

Now I'm sitting in the kitchen of your house
in Sabro, writing a synopsis for a play. I chain-write
them, all of them furious and sentimental and cen-
tered around some tragic female destiny. They sell
like hot cakes, we smile at the premiers, and we've
gotten a dog. You don't ride anymore, you sold
Frühling a long time ago. You have a ceramic work-
shop now and provide graphic design solutions for
various firms, and now you walk through our door.

The dog barks and sniffs at your crotch, you
come up to me right away and kiss me, then start
cooking; you're focused like an eagle, I could be
taming horses with my ass without you even noticing, you're that concentrated in a kitchen; you note
that I've done the dishes, but you don't see the hair
sticking up out of the sink, you don't pull on that
hair, you don't pull the beastly troll out of the drain,
a French lesbian dwarf out of the drain, you don't
buy two tablets of E from the dwarf, two doses for
us, come on, try and bite me, feel how hard I get,
listen, can you hear what I'm saying here, baby:
*Because of you I am so confused, take another little*

*piece of my heart now, please break it, take it,* I could be taming horses with my ass without you even noticing, you're that concentrated in this kitchen with its splashy plastic from 1966, I could tame the beastliest trolls, as long as I didn't break any of your West German design—that would not go un-noticed, you look after your things—last year your hands formed the two of us in clay, a pair of birds with clipped wings and limp dicks, exquisite senti-mentality, I loved that sculpture, can you remember who it was I quoted, I can't, I took a taxi to the har-bor on my own, I felt so written, so composed, oh, industry, oh, the unity of action, your heavy hands, I really thought I could be clay in those hands that night, that summer, an epic rose, prosaic ship's cargo, a peacock eye, I was completely wrong, *you're* the poetic paraphernalia in this kitchen, your big bass voice, your chest, your brown floral-patterned apron and underneath it the piercing through the fat head of your dick, is that shellfish you're pre-paring, is it something nice and tapasy, why haven't you got a cunt, the only thing you're missing is a cunt so I don't get shit on my dick and in my dick, in my urethral orifice, I'm thinking about gangrene, I'm thinking infection and rot, it keeps me awake at night, I feel guilty about it, my hygiene hysteria, it makes me passive, a paradoxical pillow-biter, I was assertive as a child, I was Bjørn with a capital *B*, I took my dad's place in bed when he moved out, you love hearing about it, it gives you mental orgasms, it's your substitute for religion, psychology:

Dad moves out, Mom screams, I'm six years old, Mom's got a dog. Mom's got a hunting dog, Mom's got a Weimaraner, Mom's got a champ, Mom's dog is named Titan. Titan's smart, Titan's sleek, Titan's got a silver coat; Titan's more than Titan, Titan's a god, an element, a moon. Titan's a wood-burning stove, Titan's a car, domestic appliances, Titan is fitness equipment, a gay porn production company, Titan's *Titan Titan*, Titan's *Titan Titan Titan*, Titan takes Dad's place in bed, Titan sleeps with Mom, Titan eats with Mom, Titan and Mom. Titan and Mom go to the World Cup in France, Titan's silver coat glistens in the sun through the trees, Titan is taken for a deer and gets shot and *dies*, Titan gets buried in the garden under the conifer, Mom weeps, I take Titan's place in bed, I sleep with Mom, I eat with Mom, me and Mom. I menstruate for the first time next to Mom, I have my first ejaculation next to Mom, I have my second, I have my fifth, my twenty-seventh, I lie flat on my stomach and rub myself against the mattress and am dog enough, man enough, woman enough, Bjørn enough for Mom. I make small incisions in my fingertips and write TITAN in blood on Mom's sheet, no, I wet my fingertips in my vagina and write TITAN in blood on the oriental rug in the living room, *I write*, I tell myself, *now I'm writing*, it makes no *sense*, but it's *valid*, so *applaud, applaud, for fuck's sake*, you love that story, you're such an easy mark, you love to visualize a blue figure eight enclosing us, you in one circle, me in the other, solar plexus protected, thereby free communication, blue soapstone under the pillow, you bore me stiff and mealy, and I still refuse to fuck you, my dick is my portfolio, my tongue is my horse.

The only time I fucked you was after a private party which I went to wearing a tight, black crushed velvet dress and an orc mask I bought at Netto, someone had tricked me and said it was a fancy dress, that I was ravishing. You smoked half a joint, a black cat of vomit came out of your mouth, I put my hand on your forehead and held you, took off the orc mask, the crushed velvet, murmuring: We're going *home*, love. I breastfed you that night, my chest swelling with gratitude as my milk squirted relief into your mouth, it was me who fucked you that night, but it was you who vomited a cat, I could tame that cat with my ass; is that saddle of venison you're preparing, is that tomato with sherry, I'm so *comfortable* in this chair, I'm so comfortable *looking* at you, I could *eat* you from here, I could *kill* you, now you're boiling something, now your ass is turned toward me, your ass is a peach, no, your ass is a nectarine, a fuck-swig of good beer, try opening a beer, try drinking that beer, try pissing on me, can't we go to the bathroom, can't you just take off that apron and piss on me, I don't think I'll ever meet another brown-eyed man who so incessantly drips pre-cum on my shriveled-up dil-don't-mind-if-I-do, I'm getting really horny now, really holistically horny, can't you just leave those vegetables, can't you just forget about that sink and piss on me, for fuck's sake, it can easily be poetic, I'm begging you, I don't want to sit here anymore, I don't want to be here anymore, can't you just / yes / yes / this is romance / it's the closest I'll ever get / it's you I love it's me who's loving it's me who's oh no I'm coming now / oh no I'm coming now oh no now no / now no now no / no / no

# DRESSUR Let A

Den / 19

Bane A - Vejledende tid: 6 min. 30 sek. (Ponyer 7 min.) - Højeste karaktersum: 290

Stævne: _____     Dommer: _____

Rytter: *Bjørn Rasmussen*

Hest: *Fragna*

| Karakter gruppe | | Øvelser | Karakter | Sum | Bemærkninger |
|---|---|---|---|---|---|
| 1 | A X | Indridning i arbejdsgalop Parade - stilstand - hilsen - arbejdstrav | 4 | 4 | tidl brat |
| 2 | C MRXV V | Højre volte Middeltrav Arbejdstrav | 6 | 10 | starter for dr. |
| 3 | A LR | Vend ad midterlinien Schenkelvigning for venstre schenkel | 5 | 15 | skyder skulder |
| 4 | C P | Volte (10 m diameter) | 6 | 21 | lidt for stor |
| 5 | HSXP | Middeltrav | 7 | 28 | godt |
| 6 | A LS | Vend ad midterlinien Schenkelvigning for højre schenkel | 4 | 32 | sid lige skyder skulder |
| 7 | C | Volte (10 m diameter) | 6 | 38 | lidt for stor |
| 8 | MXK K | Fri trav Arbejdstrav | 7 | 45 | markér overgan |
| 9 | A | Parade - 4. sek. stilstand Fremadridning i arbejdstrav | 5 | 50 | skæv g. |
| 10 | FXH H | Fri trav Arbejdstrav | 6 | 56 | |
| 11 | C | Parade - 4 skridt tilbage - middelskridt | 7 | 63 | |
| 12 | MRXVK K | Fri skridt Middelskridt | 2 | 6 12 | 75 | rid stille |
| 13 | A AC | Arbejdsgalop til venstre Slangegang - 3 buer - 1. og 3. bue i retvendt - 2. bue i kontragalop | 2 | 77 | konta'i ansving changeres (VRS) |
| 14 | HSXP PFA | Middelgalop Arbejdstrav | 5 | 82 | ej vist |
| 15 | A AC | Arbejdsgalop til højre Slangegang - 3 buer - 1. og 3. bue retvendt - 2. bue i kontragalop | 5 | 87 | lidt vild |
| 16 | MRXV VKA | Middelgalop Arbejdstrav | 7 | 94 | vænder op. |
| 17 | A FXH Før H HC | Arbejdsgalop til venstre Fri galop Afkortning til arbejdsgalop Arbejdstrav | 6 | 100 | lidt mat |
| 18 | C MXK Før K KA | Arbejdsgalop til højre Fri galop Afkortning til arbejdsgalop Arbejdstrav | 5 | 105 | slår fra |
| 19 | A L | Vend ad midterlinien Arbejdsgalop til højre | 5 | 110 | lidt slinger |
| 20 | G | Parade - stilstand - hilsen | 7 | 117 | gan g. |
| | | Udridning i skridt for lange tøjler | | 125 | |
| 1 | | GANGARTER (frihed og regelmæssighed) | 2 | 6 12 | 129 | |
| 2 | | SPÆNDSTIGHED (fremadsøgning, sving, bæring og afskub) | 2 | 6 12 | 141 | |
| 3 | | LYDIGHED (opmærksomhed og tillid, smidighed og lethed ved overbarnes udførelse, accept af biddel og lethed på sejlen) | | 5 10 | 151 | |
| 4 | | RYTTERENS OPSTILLING OG SÆDE samt korrekthed i anvendelsen af hjælpen | 2 | 5 10 | 161 | styr dit temperiment |
| Point | | | | 161 | |
| Fradrag | | | | 0 | |
| Sum | | | | 161 | |
| | | | | 161 | |

# FLOWER

I was already older when a man came up to me one day in the lobby of a public place. You're still ravishing, I said, and pulled his tie, but you're ten years too late, we can't be lovers, monogamy is an institutional shithouse, coupling an overhyped bestseller, blind to its own fiction. But let's go outside and smoke, the heat in here is oppressive, so many people.

I think of this picture often, I still see it in my mind, though I've never talked about it. Or maybe I did? Did I tell you about the cold metal in the flesh, the cut-lines in the ball sack, glowing red, glistening, now with night piss, now with salt water, grains of sand. Look, here I am, posing on a beach in a yellow bathing suit, waving.

This I know: I groomed the mare; I ate in a cold kitchen with the Brothers, the Mother. Her jaw— clack clack.

What did you eat? Medister sausage and stewed kale. What did the Brothers look like? Fair-haired, grubby.

What was your relationship with the Mother at this point? I was her son.

And you slept in the same bed as her? Yes.

Did she ever touch you? Of course she did.

But did she ever touch you *down there*? Of course she did.

And she did so at that time, when you were, how old, eleven?

What does age matter, what *is* it even? I consider the Mother's body while she sleeps—she is unconscious with grief. I smooth a finger over the long scar from the Caesarean, the shorter scar from the appendectomy, I pinch the cellulite in her thighs: what man has loved them, what man has run his fingers through her bushy black pubes, what man?

He lives in a flat in Lemvig.

He is married to a woman with a dirty blonde bob cut, pink leisure suit, lipstick, showy jewelry, rings on her fingers—jade and gold.

I call her The Lady. The Lady plays golf and bridge, and chain-smokes menthol cigarettes. The Lady retracts her upper lip when eating steak tartare so that it may remain untouched by raw egg, red meat, so that in tandem with her lower lip, un-blemished and pristine, it may shape a *darling* or a *sweetheart*, so that her lips may collude to kiss the Man softly and with gloss.

The Man was once a soldier.

The Man has no soul.

The Man is a bastard.

This I know.

I'm on the bus—the 491 to Fjaltring.

In my pocket is a contractual agreement, a copy typed by my own hands. The typewriter lacks the section sign, so in each instance I've typed the word itself. Section 1: You are to do as I tell you. Section 5: You are to report every time you mastur-bate. Section 27: You must never reveal my name. These are the instructions.

I didn't cry. He was careful. He massaged my anus for more than an hour, licking, lubricating, enlarg-ing, before finally penetrating. Mostly I wondered if I was clean enough inside; excrement is repulsive when expelled from the body, like blood or vomit; it's the stench of the homeless, a dead boy's flower. But I didn't cry.

His thick, hard dick penetrated my sphincter and probed deep into my dark shaft. A single seamless movement that didn't stop until I felt his thighs, his taut testicles against my buttocks.

Then the horses sang.

I should return to the Mother. She walks the asphalt road, hugging the ditches, embraced by her chorus of dogs, a semicircle of silver-gray. She assumes so many forms, now in the raven's purple-black, now in a coat of stiffened mud. The dogs dress her in these garments, and more follow. The rough-haired pointers strike out after midnight, returning home with cock pheasants in gaping jaws, a branch from the birch, coats smeared with kelp, saliva dribbling from their beards. The silver-gray Weimaraners sit erect in the tower room with hind legs crossed, sewing with long threads and gleaming needles until dawn arrives and the sounds of the Mother's presence trickle down the halls, water as it boils, egg as it breaks, her patchy wisps of hair that crackle electric. The Little One hears all this but remains in bed, burrowing blissfully into the dizzying white of the soft bedclothes. The house's bark creaks in the late summer wind, a rush of conifers outside in the garden, horses snorting in the stable, an expectation of grain, molasses, silage, ever honored. For they must never be disappointed, but rewarded for their toil-some industry, this is the alliance, a tacit and confidential agreement between animal and human.

The Little One spends half of each day with the mare, washing her, grooming her, feeding her. He is beguiled by how much she understands of what he feels. She presses her muzzle against him and keeps it there while he picks her mane and brushes her forehead, and when he sits down in the manger she lowers her head to him and he allows her to sniff all around his neck and throat, up and down the length of his face. He saddles her and rides toward the sea. They gallop across the stubble fields, froth bubbling in the corners of her mouth; and then the murmur of waves, that monotonous, curling swell, the sea gulping breath before unfolding smoothly onto the beach. He makes camp on the dunes, the mare standing untethered, nibbling the lyme grass, attentive to his slightest gesture. At night he rides naked into the waves. When the mare begins to swim he grips her mane tightly and leans forward to lie along her spine. Her forelegs thrust a rhythm; the glaze of the moon, the milky sea, the particles that shimmer around her coat.

The Mother's grief over the Loved One grew into a nasty great poisonous flower. The flower took up all the oxygen and its thorns tore up her inner organs; it was self-pollinating and gruesome, it was seed capsules, stamens, stalk, and stem. The boy looked after the flower, he cut it back and boiled soup from its leaves and served the soup to the Mother and the Brothers in the fragile Argentine porcelain so fabled through the generations. The boy's fingers were slender and green, he slept next to the Mother on waterproof sheets, pink and cobalt-blue in turn, each soaked with his urine in the morning, his red thighs itching and burning; the Mother washed and wrung the stained duvet cover without so much as a twitch of her nose or an eyebrow raised. The thought of her Loved One was a small soft hammer that thumped against her temple every thirty seconds, the squealing in her brain fluctuated in volume, but was constantly present. Her only relief was in the sounds of the horses in the warm stable, the chomping of hay between their jaws, the pressing of muzzles against the troughs, the snorting. The Little One baked bread and cake endlessly: cinnamon swirls, chocolate crunch, various pastries. The Brothers stuffed themselves, their bellies grew fat on all the sugar, whole-wheat flour, sticky butter; they grew big and slobbish, and the Little One observed them and marveled. The Mother didn't touch a crumb, but withered away to the bones, her scales were like snowflakes in the bed, her sex as dry as dust; he did not touch it, but *stared* his way through the nights, tireless in the single thought: That's where it *happens*, that's where the sperm *belongs*.

There's a document saved on my computer, its name is: *Bjørn has a body*. I use it to keep a catalogue of my body's ingestions and excretions: crispbread, avocado, black tea, urine. I note down my bodily business: enema, tooth brushing, beard trimming. I strive to archive the facts—there's nothing at all romantic about it, the idea is simply to carve a template.

Where are your cuts located? What is the extent of your wounds, their length and breadth? What do your cuts contain? A: necrosis. B: exposed tissue. C: pus. What do the edges of your cuts look like? A: macerated. B: inflamed. C: eczematous. D: pigmented. Is the sensitivity of your tissue satisfactory? Is the function of your superficial and perforator veins satisfactory?

I see now that when I was very young, thirteen or fourteen years old, my face was a herald of what alcohol has done to me since. The depression at the root of the thumb, used for the brief storage of salt in conjunction with the ingestion of tequila, is called the anatomical snuffbox. My anatomical snuffbox is especially deep. I can hold eight glasses of aquavit between my ten fingers: aniseed, orange, plum, bramble, dill, juniper, cole, lady's bedstraw.

The Little One gets off the bus and goes into the convenience store. The Mother has given the Little One some money for candy and the movie he is supposed to be going to with his riding instructor, but the Little One and the riding instructor won't be eating candy and watching a movie, because the riding instructor is not the Little One's riding instructor but the Loverman, because the Little One is no longer the Little One but what, what. What wants to buy a bottle of wine for the Loverman, but which is What to choose; What wants to buy cheese and grapes; What wants to buy the whole store for the Loverman, but What goes over to the videos, What pores through the modest selection, What reads the blurbs, What can't remember what What reads and must read it again, What turns the boxes over and

over in his hands, What cannot remember what
What, what the sea, what the house and the wine,
no, the candy, no, the next bus home, yes, home, no,
the wine, yes, the wine and the dick and

What are you supposed to do with love, spunky and
spirited one day, keeled over the next, head in the
gutter and puking up blood. You rinse your blue eyes
and hold out the vomit in your hand: look at this.
You batter yourself, then flatter yourself for comfort,
you yawn, curl your lips around a corn cob, sink your
teeth in, cuddle a kitten in your lap, squint at the sun,
watch as it balances on the horizon: farewell.

I get off the bus and go out to the railing. Out
into the yard. Into the convenience store. Down
to the beach. Something comes tearing toward me
and knocks me flying. It's a dog. It's only a dog,
two dogs. Then, as I get to my feet and brush the
sand off my knees, someone takes a photograph.
The dogs barge against my thighs, flicking drool
around their ears, I'm standing, hunched in a pair
of blue swim trunks, yellow swim trunks, glancing
cagily at the photographer, guilty. I turn and wade
out into the sea.

I'm interested in death by drowning. I imagine hearing a quiet hymn as the water washes through the respiratory tract and fills me up: hawthorn and elderberry, calamus and Scotch rose, willow. Tansy and crowberry, yarrow, rowan. Sloe. Cranberry. Walnut.

They come home with the dead Weimaraner in a blanket.

It's Titan, says Eddie. It was an accident.

I grip the Mother's shoulders: Who did it? Who fired the shot? She sees that I'm wearing a dress and am smeared with soot. She smiles. She puts her chubby arms around me.

That night I find collars and leashes and take two rough-haired pointers and the pistol with me.

Didn't I mention the pistol?

Well, one day two policemen were standing in the yard asking the Mother if her youngest son was dead.

Who, Bjørn? No, he's in the kitchen drawing.

What was I drawing? Horses, most likely. The mare's asshole, or maybe the trombone. And yes, after that she went out and got herself a pistol.

Did she show me the pistol? Yes, she did.

It was just too American, I suppose, too absurd a secret to keep to herself.

The Mother is veiled in black, she makes a long speech, her cold voice borne along by the wind blowing in the trees; she quotes Blixen, Brorson; the Brothers serve eggnog in smoke-colored glasses. Later, the guests gather around the long table; white candles in seven-armed candlesticks, silver cutlery, the linen napkins from Argentina. A meal is served of roasted pigeon, pheasant, fallow deer, and smoked turkey, an exuberance of meat in every shade of red, brown, and gray; and in the middle of the broad table is the glass coffin containing the boy's pasty blue flesh: lips and eyelids, breasts. During dessert—port wine, lemon mousse with blackberries—the riding instructor gets to his feet.

Look at him.

He's the one I love.

I would so much like to describe his physique, his dark eyes, his pronounced jaw, but seen from here in the coffin he seems suddenly like a stranger, so haggard and thin. Does the glass distort his stature?

He taps his silver spoon against his dessert plate, twice, three times, unfolds a typewritten sheet of paper, and does he not seem to shrink as the words leave his mouth, do his words not appear to bind his formerly so towering frame in a knot? They seem almost to weep from his mouth:

I want a man to love / a Manday to put on my shoes / a sugar cube for my stallion // Remember last year how / we spun our fists together / into a new kind of troll, a position of trust // Your tattooed shoulder / was the opposite / of fear.

# I THINK WE CAN HAVE
# A WONDERFUL FUTURE

I think of the horses as a tragic Greek chorus. They sing in the night. I imagine the rigid hierarchy disintegrating and them becoming a single will, a single warm-blooded song; polyphonic, harmonious, imponderable.

I wake up and wash my face; I put conditioner in my discolored hair, rub soap into my armpits, anus, genitals, and feet. I brush my teeth and rinse the conditioner out of my hair, the drain is clogged with hair and crud; I turn off the tap and wrap my lower body and hair in towels, scrape down the walls, dry the floor, roll deodorant under my arms, and rub lotion into my face. Then the contact lenses, one at a time, then mascara and a sanitary pad, panties and a high-waisted skirt, a scoop-neck sleeveless top, a cardigan in synthetic fiber, heeled sandals, hair in a bun with pins to keep it up.

I am in a chrysalis. I'm not sure anymore if

I'm going to hatch; I've got this feeling I'm never going to get out.

Sometimes I get this suffocating feeling in my chest and need to leave the classroom, dash for the bushes behind the playfields, and stuff handfuls of snow into my mouth. The girls in my class have gotten into the habit of gouging their forearms with drafting compasses; some guy's initials, stars, hearts. I have thoughts about cutting my face up so people can see that I'm just as ugly on the outside as I feel on the inside.

I was going to go for a little walk outside tonight before bed; I felt so cooped up and sick. I grind to a halt in the hall, at the window, at the image in the mirror: there I am again. I'm a trashy sense organ, the flapping of a bird. I'm a small raisin on a certain gentleman's desk, next to that person's wallet, that person's keys. I'm a bleeding stomach, I am a mollusk swallowed by a whale. I'm a wizened old baby, a boy-cunt, I am a sumptuous sheath, I am the sounds in the eyes of the night; I burn myself blind, there's nothing to be done about it, I don't own the rights to my body. That's me singing on your messages at night, me staining your flight suit;

if I take the car and drive to Fjaltring, will you let me in, will you make me stand there in the snow? In my bare feet?

This holiday is going to kill me.

Your letter just came, the one about swimming in the sea in winter, about bacteria. And your ultimatum. The answer is unambiguously yes, I'll stop cutting myself, I'll do anything for you, I mean it, the contract still holds and I'll stop right away, of course I will.

I was so glad to read your letter that I started to cry. I haven't cried since I was one of the little kids at school, since my first pony died, did I tell you about my first pony? It had a golden coat and an unpleasant temperament, it bit me a few times and drew blood. When they found out why, it was too late, it died of starvation, a cancerous tumor in its mouth, the bolt gun to its head. I came home early from school and saw it lying there dead in the yard, a monument of meat, blowflies shimmering in its coat. I think this was when my hatred of my mother accelerated, this string through my nervous system, constantly swelling, voluminous and vibrating, I stopped eating in sympathy with that pony, I fasted in deference to its unpleasant temperament, I didn't speak for several days.

I'm telling you, I don't think you realize how strong I am, how invincible with your black glove in my maw. And yet there's this fear somewhere outside my field of vision, trying to tell me something, what do you think it is? I slashed your saddle on purpose, of course I did, I possess a tireless longing to get myself into trouble—you know that—but I never dreamed you would ignore me, you must never do that again. And while we're at it, I think we need to make the consequences for any disobedience, forgetfulness, or laziness on my part more severe. I don't know how much is up to me, but just as an example I saw a TitanMen movie that takes place in a stable, and in one of the scenes a boy gets whipped by two muscular men who then piss in his wounds.

I don't think we should be afraid of cliché.

I think we can have a wonderful future.

Love, Bjørn.

I've only slept an hour. It's my thoughts, they keep tapping at my skull like they want out, tapping like angry fingers on an old-fashioned typewriter. Listen: the best way to learn the topographic anatomy of the human organism is by dissection, systematically exposing the structures of individual regions layer by layer with the aid of appropriate instruments. And bacteria are found in great numbers on a person's skin and mucous membranes, and most cuts will therefore become contaminated with bacteria; many of the bacteria that passively enter the cut will be unable to thrive in their new environment and will quickly perish, whereas others will feel at home and begin to multiply, and thereby colonize the cut, fuck yes.

Wrong canter, more forward, good walk, well ridden, precise. He gave marks and comments to each horse and rider—his soft, fleshy lips, the deep bass of his voice, his tongue—I took pains to write down every word on the judging score sheets. I've got such lovely handwriting, such lovely breasts, that's what he says, that's what he said, sitting in front of the fireplace in Fjaltring fondling them, pressing the fat bulb of his index finger against my nipples, that's when he said so.

But anyway, this dressage event, I'd been having this argument with Eddie about who got to be scribe: I'm the youngest, I yelled at him, I ride the most, I'm district now, you can run the food stall, you can add up the points: 6, 6, 7.

So we were sitting in the judge's box, partially hidden from view. He filled out his body to the point of bursting, he was a suit of armor, a hoof in the head wouldn't have rattled him. I was a child. Trembling, infatuated, totally oblivious to everything, totally in thrall to my mindless obsession—a spineless, slobbering stupidity. I would have put anything at all on those score sheets. If he'd said, *You're seated like a pile of shit*, I would have penciled the words in the space for position and seat; if he'd said, *Dance me to the end of love, forever*, I'd have noted it down under leg-yields; if he'd said, *I love you*. But he didn't say that. He said: rhythm, suppleness; nice, round volte; 5, 6, 4.

As a new horse and rider enter the arena I put my hand on his chaps-clad thigh, but he removes it immediately. During the canterwork I do it again and he leaves it there. My hand moves slowly to his crotch, his dick growing erect under the thick leather, a hard, hot sensation burning inside me, a taut, quivering string extending from knee to perineum, spine, temples. My stomach becomes a centrifuge. Free fall.

Rider and horse leave the arena to applause and I come in my pants. Left hand on his crotch, right hand holding the pencil, ready to write down the overall scores: 6/12, 7/14.

During my own test on Magna an hour later, I get my comeuppance, Eddie's neat cursive spelling it out: H showing some tension, not tracking, shoulder falling out. Weak, abrupt, sit still, keep your head. I lose the class, it's unfair, absurd, I go straight up to him and demand an explanation. I don't get one, all he says is Eddie's scribing the rest of the classes, Eddie smirks at me, all chocolate-milk moustache, then bites the end off of a red sausage. I feel like puking. I have no idea what I'm doing with this clown.

Believe nothing of what I say about feelings. I only have the rudiments of anything genuine. And if anything genuine does come along, it always falls to pieces: talk to me about implosion, about atoms. You chase a frog for hours and when finally you get your hands around it, it dies of shock. And if I really get you someday, I won't want you anymore. I'll want something else instead. What. Tell me the difference between want and need—I don't think there is one. What is there then. Capitalism, talk to me about capitalism. No, human nature. Oh, listen: it's black as night inside my ass; inside my ass, about 6 cm up, there's an erogenous zone equivalent to the clitoris or the head of your dick. Fact. When this point is touched, vibrations go through the spine, the hammer, the stirrup, and listen: the asshole is dialectical, the asshole is a dead man's flower, a dead woman's flower, the asshole is a fugue, a theme with variations; feelings, on the other hand…frogs, mothers, riding instructors, and feelings, they're the same old story. Suck my plot.

We went to the sea yesterday. Mom was draped in black, except for her aubergine headscarf. She insisted on sitting in the back seat even though I'm not supposed to drive; the rusty yellow Volvo made a racket, we had to shout if there was anything we wanted to say to each other, but there wasn't; I concentrated on shifting gears, on making it fluid, the engine would stall at the slightest thing. We followed the path to the top of the dunes, it was edged with lyme grass. The sea was a froth of white, Mom's scarf flapped in the wind, she had to keep it in place with one hand, I took the other and gave it a squeeze. Then I left her and went inside the bunker.

The bunker is silent, cool, and dark, I have to get on my knees to crawl all the way in. Suddenly,

I'm gasping for air at the thought of a sandslide burying the entrance, closing the cracks, killing the last slivers of light.

It's him, crawling in after me.

In the heart of the bunker he grabs me, presses me against the cold wall, his breathing heavy and excited, his hard hands everywhere, in my hair, my eyes, around my throat, his teeth, his tongue in my ear, he can hardly breathe.

I see people on the beach through the embrasures; they're out for a walk by the sea, they're sunbathing, their kids are splashing in the waves, their dogs. I notice my mother. She's posing in a yellow, a blue, bathing suit, big sunglasses, she shakes her hair and laughs. The man taking her photograph is wearing small white shorts. He turns toward us.

As he puts the camera to his eye you come inside me. You squirt your load, three hard thrusts, five hard thrusts. You remain inside me, withdrawing only when your dick has gone limp, only when it's finished, only it's not finished. The man stands there with his camera in front of his face.

I'd happily die in a trench with you at my side.

I'd happily explode in the mud.

I shake uncontrollably just seeing your car on the gravel out front. There's a videotape in the glove compartment with my name on it, the disclosure of our affair is only a breath away, if anyone should find that tape, oh, if anyone finds it. There are your black gloves and a videotape in the glove compartment, there are rear seats of white leather. And then there's me. In the trunk. In a golf bag. When you stop off in Lemvig to buy groceries, you open the trunk wide so anyone passing can see me, raise the alarm, throw me in the sea.

Have I mentioned Lemvig? Lemvig is Happyville, West Jutland. In Lemvig no one gets called their rightful name. In Lemvig they call you Asshole and Fuckface, Keld the Cunt, Karate-Arne. Nigger John, Jannie the Slut, Lajla the Corpse, Fairy Mikael, the Paki, the Paki's sister, the Paki's uncle, and when the clock strikes darkness *Uncle Lemvig* comes out into the stubble field above the town and pours his spud water into your pale mouth. We're not talking traditional dictatorship here, we're not hanging Uncle Lemvig's portrait on the wall over the dining table, we're talking invisible embedments of root, of belonging, *core*, the desired effect can be revealed by the eyes: Is there any *substance* in him, is she *natural*. If you're a man in Lemvig and you fondle another man's *lem*, which is a dick, in Lemvig, or if you put it in your mouth or your anus, barflies in the vicinity will be compelled to produce thick feces for the disobedient culprit to swallow. Likewise, any woman wearing a veil may be unveiled by any means and her black hair shorn in the manner of close-cropped women who have never touched a *lem*, which is a dick, in Lemvig, and who must by necessity be aided in such an endeavor. In the event that these poor stray souls refuse to accept our outstretched hand and continue to offend before the eyes of our children, severe means may be implemented, certain measures taken. For verily there is root, and root *hurts*, and root is *good*, and root shall be upheld, and the *functionality* of root shall be upheld, and *being local, being from 'round here* shall be upheld and never yielded, but show its true *lem*, which is a dick, and therefore a queer *lem*, which is a dick, must perforce be severed at the root and tossed into the harbor; therefore a black, veiled cunt must perforce be fucked to shreds by wrinkly old white men and tanned muscular youngsters on a night in late summer in a back alley of Lemvig, as sure as eggs is eggs, I speak from experience, from the stubble field at the hour of darkness, oh dear old uncle spudshit, burn my lips in shame, burn my boyish, blushing apple cheeks, they are ripe and ready, now let them burst, SPLAT SPLAT, oh big fat uncle-snake, start up your harvester and split me apart, *s'il vous plait*.

This is a procedure, a stuffing of the anus. I haven't had a pulse since I was an embryo, I haven't had a heart since I aborted it; if only I could sleep. Of my hundred origins, not one do I believe. My sperm has no validity, my sperm is useless to anyone, my sperm provides no joy, no benefit. I no longer feel anything for you after I had you that one last time, how shitty if it got me knocked up, if it has I shall be forced to laugh and go back to Lemvig and pay someone to kick me in the stomach and get rid of it, get rid; or maybe not even as far as to Lemvig, for in its hinterland too there are so many assholes looking for a bit of fun; fuck, if I ever see you again I'll make sure you never reach your birthday ever again, and strangle you with that flag of yours.

I open my eyes, mouth dry, sore throat, scratched my cheek in my sleep. Remove the tampon I've worn all night, waves of pain in my stomach. Rust-colored urine, hard excrement tinged with green, I poke my ears with Q-tips, clean my teeth with thin floss, brush them with a hard toothbrush, put my contact lenses in. Sand, grit, clay, crust, and collapsing soil, drums and bass and piano, fields, forests, motorway, short-crust pastry. The kneading made me sweat, flour between my toes in high-heeled sandals, and my high-piled heart, it beats once a second, when I'm still.

I'm still.

So vocal.

I light a cigarette and inhale, flash my left ankle. Such a delicate ankle, so smooth and ready, okay, okay, string section then.

The reason I haven't written anything in this book for such a long time is partly that I haven't had a single thought that made sense. I don't know why I tell myself I've got to make sense, I really think I need to get away from here, I've started cutting myself again. He hasn't been here in four months, he's moved Frühling, whose tail I cut off at the root. Tonight I swam alone in the sea, the air was phosphorescent, I drank gin and gin, I yelled until I was hoarse, now I'm hoarse, now I'm empty, I'm so empty, I'm so tired, I don't think I'll write in you anymore, I don't trust you, I think Eddie's been in here rummaging, I think Mom's giving me funny looks, is it my mouth.

I went to the Rom Riding Club last night, I sat on a round bale of silage and watched his lesson, ate fries and drank synthetic raspberry juice with Line and Karina. I took the picture out of my bag, a photo of a dick, a black man's big stiff dick, I printed it from his computer, I told them, and pointed at him in the arena, I printed it from his computer. Then I told Line and Karina that he's been fucking me for more than a year and I'm out of my head because of it, I love him so desperately I want to die, and that was why I was there. They went totally silent. I showed them my cuts and scars and explained to them that I've been harming myself for months in the name of love.

I cut myself, I slice myself, I tear myself. I tear at my hair, I pull my hair from my scalp, eyebrows, pubic hair, I bite my nails to the quick, fingers, hands. I hit myself with my fists or with hard objects, I pound my head against a wall, I squeeze out imaginary blackheads, I scratch my sores and infect them, I prevent the sores from healing. I burn myself with cigarettes, a lighter, boiling water. I do it with razor blades, a scalpel, a knife, broken glass, a pair of drafting compasses, jewelry, with plastic knives and forks, broken plates, the sharp edge of a debit card or CD, I do it to my wrists and forearms, chest, legs, face, and genitals. I do it criss-cross, fine patterns, parallel lines, *X*s and symbols and words; I cut his name into my flesh, here he is, bleeding, we love each other, we devour each other. We agree on a code word before having sex, it's important to choose a word that has nothing to do with sex and can't be misunderstood, this we know; don't choose a word like *no* or *stop* or *don't*, these words might be part of the game and the fantasy of having something done to you that you don't want done to you. Words like *circus* and *orange* are good words, and used the world over, and when we lick ass we're aware that the secretions of the rectum may contain small amounts of blood, this is why eating feces is risky, but on the other hand there's no risk in shit getting on the skin unless there are open sores or scratches.

Yes. That's what I said. That's how I kept on, kept on until I puked; dick and Line in love, computer and crazy Karina, French fries and death. Yes.

# LITTLE BJØRN

I think Bjørn availed himself of the Mother's rattling old yellow Volvo in order to slip away. On the morning he left, he went into the dog pen and shot the Weimaraners. He flayed the skins, sewed them together crudely, and wrapped himself in the clownish cloak of dog hides, fur stained with blood, speckles of silver-gray. A head hung from his shoulder, another dangled at his heart like a mutant breast, claws danced at his knees and hips. He buried the headless corpses next to their father, Titan, beneath the conifer, they barely filled the hole, small aborted calves, bone and slop. He fetched three bucketfuls of ash from the fireplace and emptied them on top. Then he went to the stable. In the hay loft he found the hidden afterbirth of the mare quivering with decay. He bound the gluey, black-red pudding to his head like a hood, twining the umbilical cord about his neck.

The riding instructor was sitting in the

yellow upholstered armchair when the Little One entered and said: You've been silly. But I've been silly too. You must forgive me.

The riding instructor made no reply, the Little One went on: I've made up my mind. I'm leaving. I intend to enter the twenty-first century in a different town, I intend to enter my eighteenth year as a different person.

The riding instructor said nothing. He was looking down at his hands.

You can open your mouth and say goodbye. If you do, it'll be the last time I see you. Or you can come with me. I love you.

The riding instructor said nothing. But he raised his eyes and looked at the Little One, who stepped closer, swallowed, and said again: I love you.

With that, the riding instructor got to his feet, walked five paces, six paces toward the door of the bedroom, placed his hand on the door handle, turned and looked at the Little One, and said: Farewell, Bjørn. Farewell.

# BJØRN, A BAGFUL OF BACTERIA

When Bjørn became a grown-up he could no longer speak. Born into a masculine world, a feminine world, he had no language of his own. The only thing he could do was to read masculine texts, feminine texts that were not his own. He rented a room in the capital, lay down on a mattress, and read. When it got dark and he needed a lamp, there was none to be found. And so he went out.

In a blues bar, he met a middle-aged chanteuse who stood by the piano and sang:

In a time when horses rot and the family sucks / rarely does my heart stand still, still and open in snow and clamorous sound / after twenty-seven hours in the sun / I'm still pale, pudgy, and ice-cold inside // In a time when I'm too ugly and vulnerable to venture out / rarely do I throw up, throw myself toward another / after twenty-seven years in prison / still we lick each other's stamps...

The chanteuse had previously been a man. Now she was busty and wearing a raspberry-colored miniskirt. Her hair was a bluster of curls and red, red hair and red-wine lips, she chain-smoked cigarettes and commented immediately on Bjørn's scars, which were visible up and down the lengths of his arms, he was in a sleeveless white undershirt. Bjørn wrote down some words in big, awkward capitals on a napkin and pushed it toward her: I WANT WORK.

Of course you do, said the busty one, you can work for me. I'm writing my memoirs and need a secretary, a scribe who asks no questions, *I do the talking*; language gives me the biggest orgasms, can you type?

I'm saying it the way it is, the way it sounds.

Bjørn works for the Lady in a suburb four days a week. He weeds the Lady's garden, tends the Lady's roses, writes down the Lady's memoirs as she dictates.

Bjørn buys a lamp, a radio, a TV, a computer, and a newspaper subscription. Bjørn buys raspberry tarts and gin, chili with chicken, avocados and cauliflower.

Bjørn creates an online profile, two profiles,

five: Bjørn perspires. Bjørn enjoys Danish peas and watermelon in pleasant company. To think that Bjørn can get so red. Bjørn has pain in his back. Bjørn rows a marathon. Bjørn ingests tainted meat and goes down with the squirts. Bjørn says thanks a zillion for all your lovely messages. Bjørn is ready, set, raring to be an adult. Bjørn just got inked. Bjørn is OMG over his brother getting straight $A$s in the artificial insemination of pigs. Get a load of Bjørn holding a big motherfucking lobster. So, that's the garden furniture treated for the season, look how the wood just loves it. Another weekend gone before you know it.

Bjørn goes online, Bjørn goes for a walk, Bjørn goes around the garden, picking some blackberries and hemlock, and the years go too. Bjørn turns on the TV and is kept informed as to the way he talks:

My mental hang-ups are history. When on rare occasions I start doubting myself because of injustices in the world or a downturn in the economy, I go fetal in an egg of pure white light and cleanse my nervous system of foreign bodies.

We must ensure that parallel societies do not establish themselves in our cerebellum. If you can't find your core, start looking. It's the size of a soccer ball or a child's head.

If you find it hard to describe the way you perceive yourself, try writing a letter to someone who means something to you, your partner for instance, your children, your god, or just your own body:

Dear body. Firstly, the ideal of you being in great shape and fully intact is cultural. It doesn't hold in all cultures at all times, it doesn't hold for circumcision, it doesn't hold for cranial deformation in ancient Egypt, it doesn't hold for the binding of women's feet in China, or for the piercing of the ear, nose, navel, and genitals, for example. The female Mursi of Ethiopia slit their lower lips and insert into them increasingly larger clay discs in order to make themselves more attractive for marriage. Some Central African tribes use rings to elongate the neck until eventually they are unable to bear the head without. Odin gave up an eye for wisdom, Buddha gave flesh from his body to a hungry tiger, the religious Flagellants of the fourteenth century mortified their flesh by whipping themselves. Tooth extraction, trepanation, self-infliction of wounds, and the mutilation of the genitals are socially sanctioned in numerous cultures—religious people the world over penetrate their hands and feet in identification and solidarity with the sufferings of Jesus.

In the late nineteenth century, reports flooded in of needle girls: doctors would find hundreds of needles in their bodies, as well as glass shards and splinters, drawing pins, shoe nails.

That said, I'm not an ancient Egyptian with a Chinese woman's feet, an Ethiopian lower lip, a Central African neck. I'm not Odin, nor am I Buddha, and I'm no needle girl either, this I know. My skin is my largest organ, my skin is an elastic covering that encases the entire body, read: you. Yours is not the body of the horse, the hound, the reptile, or the bird either. The skin of the turkey is covered by feathers, the mare's by fur, the crocodile's by horny scales. The crocodile has no bladder and no urinary tract, so excrement and urine are expelled simultaneously via the so-called cloaca. The adder, boiled or as an ingredient in soup, may play an important role in relieving a variety of afflictions such as dry mouth, increased salivation, stomach pains, constipation, nausea, vomiting, diarrhea, stomach and intestinal bleeding, bleeding into the skin, swelling of the mucous membranes, a heightened tendency toward perspiration, rapid pulse, skin rashes, itching, coughing, tinnitus, headaches, dizziness, blurred vision, darkened vision, breathing difficulties, arrhythmia, high blood pressure, low blood pressure, raised liver enzyme count, joint pain, fever, involuntary muscle spasms, muscular stiffness, tremors, agitation, anxiety, reduced awareness, memory lapses, hallucinations, fainting.

Bjørn has a dream about love between human beings. He imagines two people making love to each other. The people manifest themselves as the Lady and Bjørn, two beautiful young lovers in a colorful silent movie called *Stretched Meat*:

Bjørn opens all the windows and cleans the entire apartment. The dishes haven't been washed for a week, she hasn't been out once, she's been living on hyphens and tea, dark rum and crispbread with avocado; looking humans in the eye is easy when you never see a soul. But what about the Lady, does the Lady have a soul? Not if you ask her— what would she want a soul for, she's got enough as it is, she's got this entire brisk, brilliant, and angular twenty-something-year-old body. See the Lady's legs cross the street, see her faded, washed-out T-shirt, her slender digit loops a strand behind her ear, the right ear, the slightly protruding, pierced ear, see her butterfly earring as it dangles, blue and bronze and blank as a mirror, see her emerald-green painted eyelids, her white front teeth biting into the fullness of her pink lower lip, see her thumbs upon the cellphone: Darling, I'll be with you in fifteen minutes.

Shampoo, dental floss, toothbrushing, shaving of legs, armpits, pubic hair, Bjørn's little black hairy cunt. The Lady has a taste for it. The Lady's cunt is gorgeous, big and red, inner labia hanging exposed, an infuriatingly delightful turkey, a thick bush surrounding her clit. Bjørn smiles, the turquoise tile in the bathroom smiles—imagine being so debased, so deliriously *verliebt*. The Lady has been putting off her visit for a month due to exams, we're into June now, and Bjørn is compiling an ever-growing catalogue of facts, an archive of amorous conquests dedicated to the Lady, who now buzzes the intercom and is every bit as ravishing as Bjørn remembers her; she hasn't changed in the slightest, relax, relax, she's even brought flowers, pale pink lilies wouldn't you know, it's not like her at all, but she wanted to, summer's at the door and she's just gotten straight *A*s in vocal harmony, which leaves only her dissertation, and what then?

Bjørn has another dream: him riding around in West Jutland, in the city and some other place abroad, on a warmblood mare with some of himself in the saddle bag: a bagful of bacteria. For every disdained, dejected, dilapidated soul he passed, he took his bag and offered a piece of Bjørn to the damned and deserted one, who immediately upon ingestion flourished and followed on behind, and thus Bjørn rode through the landscape with an ever-increasing train of Bjørn-like figures at his rear. At every stop, they burned the flagpoles of the town to the ground, raping and mutilating and eating the propertied classes. When eventually there was nothing left in the bag, Bjørn pulled it over his head, tied the reins around his neck, and dug his spurs into the mare's flanks. The black-clad figures stood shoulder-to-shoulder in a long rank and watched him disappear over the horizon.

Bjørn penetrates an older man. The man lives in a miserable room with leather belts and chains hanging from hooks in the ceiling. The man drinks a glass of Bjørn's urine while they converse on the subject of happiness theory, which is the twenty-first century's designation for taking possession of something, for example oneself. The man wishes to give his body to Bjørn, he is willing to part with his relative superiority, they make an agreement ensuring the master/slave relationship remains intact. The man has a rose tattooed around his asshole, the thorny stem continues up his spine, ending in a little spearhead at his neck. The penetration lasts twenty-seven seconds. Bjørn receives 800 kroner, he buys a bottle of gin and a poetry collection and puts the rest away in a jar under the bed. He hums a pop song. He carries the deed to the man's sixty-year-old body in his inside jacket pocket.

Bjørn's whore name is Bjørn.

Bjørn's knight name is Bjørn.

Bjørn's artist name is Bjørn.

Bjørn's name is Bjørn. And thus, no one can expose him.

Bjørn is nearly happy. But when taking a brief shower before going to sleep he performs this secret ritual: for every new body he has involved himself with, he makes a fine incision around his left nipple. When he reaches twenty-seven incisions, he switches to the right nipple, the rays of pain are soothed by the cold water, his nipples blaze like suns, and Bjørn thinks to himself: It's for *his* sake I'm doing this, one day they'll shine on *him*.

I still don't know where Bjørn was the day the phone rang. Was he asleep? Was he totally wasted? Was he in bed next to someone's naked body? A man's body? The Lady's? Was he so far gone into sleep that he could not hear the ringtone's volume rising and rising? Was he dreaming? Had he come to terms with the thought of never seeing his Loverman again? Had he come to terms with having an indefinite mind in a definite body? Had he not cut himself in a month?

I don't know. I'm sorry. My brain is a raisin. This I know: My flesh is clothed, my rawness is cosmetic. My heart is fictionalized, the scans consistently show a blue-black spot. I am encouraged to allow an endoscopic camera to slide down my throat, and my organs are illuminated in glimpses, the way an irregularly blinking fluorescent tube throws light on a crime scene in a movie, an underground parking garage, a former bathhouse. Perform a scraping of the gastrointestinal region, give me the hum of the blender over lung and liver, over uvula and

Now I can see him. Bjørn.

He's not asleep.

He's sitting on a bus. On the seat next to

him: a duffel bag. His eyes are clear, his face is open like he's been crying. He leans his head against the bus window, outside the trees blur by, grand and majestic, are they oaks?

His phone rings.

He doesn't recognize the number. But he answers it all the same. His voice trembles. And in the midst of that tremble he realizes who it is.

It's *him*.

They're going to see each other again.

It's going to happen again.

The horses are going to sing.

Bjørn speaking. He orders his second mojito from the café bartender with the pale, aristocratic mouth, nose and eyebrow piercings, and he utters the whole *sentence* in Spanish, but has no idea what to do with his hands: they flutter from hair to mouth to arm, they count the scars again and again, two, five, fourteen, why is he acting like this? Is it because there's something big in store, because a *they* is about to break loose, a resurrection, a *once again*? Are these the final minutes before everything goes down, the turning point in his life, is that the *journey* he's about to embark on, isn't it a bit silly working oneself up like this, isn't it all going to lead to disappointment, hasn't he learned from experience, the disappointment that comes from expectation is plain for all to see on his arms and legs, chest and genitals, shouldn't he at least be holding back on the Spanish?

Bjørn speaking. He starts to laugh. He's sitting by himself, in the café's velour, and he can't stop laughing. He's been sitting there an hour and a half, fantasizing more and more riding instructor with every mojito, more and more sun-drenched future in an expensive new top that's supposed to signal integrity and openness, hide scars but show off skin. And now that skin begins to prickle on the inside of his left thigh, nearly at the groin, prickle, prickle, prickle, oh, to be so privileged as to own a body that speaks, how easily it could fall into decay and oblivion, how far his dil-don't-mind-if-I-do has traveled in these velour hours, how pledged is he to his chaps-clad, dick-pierced dreams, to calm brown-eyed oceans, the soft and only hope of a thigh, how many heavenly *besos* have dizzied his walnut brain, and now he prickles everywhere.

Bjørn walks home through the city with the cold wind at his throat. He walks for over an hour, unable to cycle in this urban configuration, he possesses not a single scarf, and what use is covering up? It all goes straight to his system: the shrill voices, battle cries, whimpers. Acrid smells of endorphins, urine, deep fat. Lit-up ads for underwear, pension schemes, it all goes to the blood, the nervous system, the cold wind is nothing by comparison.

The next day his throat is speckled with white bacteria. His mouth is grit and slime, he smokes four cigarettes and takes the S-train to the Lady's place.

Hi, gorgeous.

Can I stay here a while?

Yes, of course you can. You've got the flu, I can tell.

Bjørn is so visible in the sticks. He sits, outlined in the fog, sheathed in a fat membrane. He says this to the Lady: I feel like I'm in a bell jar, a cheese display, I can't get in touch with the world.

The Lady asks what kind of cheese he feels like. She has studied cognitive psychology and thinks you can alter the way you perceive yourself by switching cheeses. She has put a padlock on the drawer containing the kitchen knives. She has filled a bowl with substitutes: elastic bands to tighten around the wrists and snap against the skin, a red marker to look like blood. She really wants to help.

The Lady places a finger bowl of iced water next to Bjørn's plate. He takes it with him to bed and listens to her murmurings: Every bird screams with his own beak. Give him five years and a proper education.

Feta? Emmental?

## YOU AND ME

I'm writing this so I can let go of you. My life story doesn't exist, but you do, I do, this right hand, this liver. This body exists, this ludicrous turkey, this skin, so coarsely structured, the auricle so complex in relief, and with countless names, the eye has rods and cones in which color pigments are broken up in light and regenerate in darkness. And I was already older, twenty-four, twenty-five, when you came up to me one day in the lobby of a public place and made me jump.

You were wearing an olive-green shirt, top button undone—your black, curly chest hairs— tight jeans, well-worn white sneakers. Only your cropped, graying hair and the lines around your eyes said you were past forty; you'd grown a beard. Right away, I wanted to give birth to your children, I wanted your sunglasses, big and impenetrable; and my pulsating perineum, my quivering vocal cords, my awareness of imminent disintegration stank a mile off. You were a nation state, you placed your big hands on my shoulders, looked me in the eyes, and addressed me thus: you, you, you.

Line and Karina's mother collects me from the Rom Riding Club. She's a school nurse, she knows I cut myself, that I'm manipulative, hysterical, I do it for the attention, everyone knows. I've gouged a hole in my perineum just below my balls, because I want to be a girl, I want a little cunt of my own so I can get dicked in three holes at once, get knocked up and watch my belly swell and be happy. Everyone knows, the Brothers know, Line and Karina know, the school nurse knows. She puts her arms around me anyway. I'm clutching the photo of the black man's dick; it's flecked with French fry grease and ketchup.

She wants to drive me to my dad's in Lemvig. I don't have a dad, I tell her, but she insists. I stand there, eyes darting, looking for you, I'm scared you've already gone, but your car's still on the gravel over by the show arena. The front door on the driver's side is open. I find the videotape in the glove compartment and drop it in my bag. It's mine, it's got my name on it: Bjørn.

When the school nurse rings the doorbell,

the Lady answers. Her hair's dyed with henna, a dribble of egg yolk on her lip. The school nurse goes inside to speak to my dad and the Lady looks at me, tilts her head, and strokes me on the cheek.

Little Bjørn, she says. Little Bjørn.

I've got something for my dad, I tell her, and open my bag.

I hand her the video.

Then take off.

This picture: my mom in the yard in front of the farmhouse, an ecstatic look on her face—her open, trembling mouth. Dead animals in her arms; the aborted foal, the decapitated chickens, the dog, the hounds. Limbs and organs spill from her embrace, feathers, fur, blood. The eyes are collected in a bucket in my hand, the cold metal knocks against my pale, chubby legs, the pistol is heavy in the inside pocket of my oilskin coat. And then the bus I've got to catch. The thought of the last bus that night in June destroys me, I scream into my mother's face, I snatch the pistol and shove the muzzle into my mouth. My mom as she drops the animals, the fluids that stream from her. I'm cold and new.

I see you waiting for me at the bus stop outside the convenience store, the sound of the waves as they batter the beach when I get off the bus and go to you, when you throw your arms around me unexpectedly, unfathomably.

After I went outside to smoke with you, after I flicked the lighter in front of your cigarette, after you put your hand around my wrist to catch the flame with the end of your cigarette, you told me you live in the woods near Sabro, that there's a tree there that weeps, it's got this bulge across the trunk like a mouth with a harelip, and a hole a bit further up like an eye, and this eye weeps resin—thick, glistening resin that trickles down the trunk.

Nice, I said, send me a photo.

*Pupilla* is the Latin for the pupil of the eye, it means "little doll" and refers to the tiny image of the beholder that is reflected in the surface of the cornea when a person looks into another person's eyes.

And so we were, two little dolls reflected in each other's pupils. Encircled by the brown, green, yellow of our irises, the cloudy white of our orbs, crisscrossed by the tiny red filaments of our blood vessels, trails of hemorrhage in skies of snow, we were two small, cockeyed dolls, safe for a few seconds.

And you cried.

It was the last time I saw you.


What are two dolls, two hearts. When there is language between you and me. In the space between. What is a pupil, two, four, what is a contract between mucous membranes. When there is such a long way from brain to brain. What is a feeling when there are facts. When science fiction is in the space between, when in the sink there is a beastly troll. A braying specimen to boot. What is capitalism to a troll, what is natural. What is genetics, a dick, a mother.


The Brothers picked me up from the station in Struer. They patted me on the back, put their hands on my shoulders. Vilhelm was driving, his two little daughters were belted in on the back seat beside me. They were in red-and-white checked dresses with ruffles, white tights. One of them had chickenpox all over her face. We drove through Gudum, Nørre Nissum, and into Lemvig. Vilhelm pulled in at the harbor; he needed to go to the butcher's shop, the bakery, the cheese shop, the fish market;

Eddie needed to go to the pharmacy.

I lifted the girls out of the car, one on each arm, and went over to Larsen's diner. Five young men were sitting inside eating hamburgers; they were in uniform, Danish flags sewn on at the shoulder. The waitress wiped spatters of fat and relish off the counter with a damp cloth. Half a centimeter of flesh-colored hair poked out of her scalp, transitioning into a feathery helmet of piss-yellow fluff. The skin around her eyes draped onto her cheeks.

When we pulled up in front of the farmhouse, the Mother was shoveling heaps of soft excrement into a wheelbarrow. The girls ran toward her shrieking with glee, and three rough-haired pointers came bounding up and stuck their snouts under the girls' dresses. Vilhelm shouted them off, digging the toe of his rain boot in their bellies. The Mother stood there looking at me. She had this round, open wound in her throat and was missing the tips of three fingers on one hand.

Later I found out she lost them loading the horses. She had made the mistake of twisting the lunge rope around her hand, the powerful beasts had not been inclined to be slaughtered, and one of them had yanked her onto the gravel with such force her joints had given way in succession, snap, snap, snap.

Now there were only two horses left in the stable, one was the mare, she hadn't had the heart to send her to the slaughterhouse. I led the mare out of the box and tethered her by the snap hooks. Her forehead was graying now, her back sagged and her joints were stiff, she could hardly walk. I groomed her. I started at the head and worked my way back and down with the direction of her coat. I ran the body brush over the metal curry comb at short intervals, knocking the accumulated hair and dust onto the stable floor. I brushed her legs, thighs, groin, fetlocks, and mane. I picked her hooves, scraped the grit from the frog and stale fertilizer from the bars. I trimmed the feathering of her fetlocks, the hair inside her ears, the chestnuts.

I read your letter while doing the dishes, the radio playing quiet, smoochy pop: *What you gonna do with your life? When you gonna live your life right?* You tell me you've got a big orchard between the house and the woods near Sabro; apples, lemons, walnuts. You've taken on two dwarves, five dwarves, they look after the watering, the weeding;

113

they sow seeds and cut back the trees. *And there's nobody else at home.* You sleep upstairs in a space by the window so you can wake up to the deer in the mornings. *The building is empty and there's nobody else at home.*

You've included a photograph of the tree that weeps. I put it with the others in the desk drawer, take it out again, and put it on the fridge with two magnets, two letters of the alphabet in pink and cobalt-blue plastic, I take it down again.

*And in the next house. And in the next house. And in the next house. There's nobody else at home.*

I'm sitting in my kitchen writing this. I know you're in the city now, I know I can go out and find you, I can go straight to your hotel and knock on your door, maybe that's why my hands are trembling like this, maybe *that's* what love is, a nonstop state of the shakes, or maybe it's this: you reading me. In the now that is yours. Which is now. Now. Hi.

Reading "me" is of course a stupid slip of the tongue, but now that it's said I should mention that this is by no means entirely my own work. I've been ripping off sentences from all over the place: Marguerite Duras's *The Lover*, Sylvia Plath's *Journals*, Antoine de Saint-Exupéry's *The Little*

*Prince*, Kathy Acker's *Don Quixote: Which Was a Dream*, and Christine Hesselholdt's *Du, mit du*. Bo Møhl's *At skære smerten bort*, Martin E. Mathiesen and Jørgen Egeberg's *Regionær Anatomi*, *Sår* by Finn Gottrup and Lars Olsen, *Sanseorganerne og huden* by Erik Andreasen, and more. I want to thank Maria, Maria, Marie, Niels, Tine, Christel, and Solvej. Pablo, Jakob, Simon, Olivia, Mathias, Merete, and the Copydan copyright management agency. And you. Obviously.

I'm curled up in the kitchen sink writing this. I've taken up my position within this rectangle; I speak until my bones rattle. I'm twenty-seven years old, I've been a myth for such a long time, and now I'm gray flesh.

I'm curled up in the glove compartment, in the mare's manger. I'm curled up in the minibar of your hotel room and I'm going to stay here till it's time to die, by which time I shall be as old and bleached as the chocolates in your desk, the ones you offer to younger and springier chickens. And when they have gone, you'll take me out, you'll put me on your bedside table. You think you can help me, you think you can get me out of this parenthesis, but what would I do then, once I was out, tell me that.

Do you think distances can be shortened, do you honestly think my name means a thing. You want me to say it aloud, BJØRN. You want me to say it in the minibar, in the car, in bed, in the kitchen. BJØRN BJØRN BJØRN. It's a song you want, a fugue, a theme with variations, violins heralding the end, then a crashing full stop, verse, bridge, chorus, breakdown, but the slutty little clown says no, the little boy-cunt has spoken, tissue will tear.

OK, so now I'm going over to your hotel in the guise of a full-grown man, I'm going to knock on your door, and then we're leaving, we're going to drive, we're going to drive off a cliff and be split into atoms, but not until 2060, you're going to be behind the wheel and I'm going to be standing on the roof saying it the way it is, the way it sounds, or rather no, I'm going be shouting, no, howling:

WE ARE THE ELASTIC COVERING THAT ENCASES THE ENTIRE BODY

WE ARE THE SYLTE, THE SILK AND THE SATIN, WE ARE A DREAM OF GUNFIRE AND THE CHILLY HAND OF GOD AT YOUR BROW ON A HOT DAY IN JUNE, A RING, A REED, BREAD, A HEART

WE ARE A COVERED SURFACE, A CLENCHED CHALK-WHITE HAND AROUND A PROFUSION OF GLISTENING BLACK HAIR, WE PROTECT OUR

FORESKIN FROM MUTILATION WITH PAPER FLAGS, SO THAT NIGHT MAY FALL GENTLY AND INSECTS FLIT

WE ARE THE RED THIGHS THAT ITCH AND BURN, AND A BRANCH OF THE BIRCH SMEARED IN MUD, SALIVA DRIBBLING FROM OUR BEARDS, WE ARE THE OPPOSITE OF FEAR

WE ARE PINK AND COBALT BLUE, LONG-NECKED, BOILED SOUP AND A WAILING TONE, A SMALL SOFT HAMMER THUMPING AT THE TEMPLE, WE ARE THE TEXTURE OF CAESAREAN SECTION, THE STRUCTURE OF THE CELLULITE AND SNAP, SNAP, A SMALL CAPSULE OF SLEEP, INDEED, WE ARE THE PAIN-SMOTHERING ENDORPHIN, THE EROGENOUS ENKEPHALIN, A DOG-HEAD DANGLING FROM THE SHOULDER, CLAWS DANCING AT THE KNEES AND HIPS, WE ARE IMPREGNATED TURKEYS, AND THE LUNGS OXYGENATE THE BLOOD, THE LIVER, RED-BROWN AND CONE-SHAPED, THE INSTRUCTIONS ARE THIS: CONTINUE INTO FIRE AND FEATHERS FOR THE FEWEST OF SECONDS, AND THEN THE END

WE ARE THE FUCK-DOLL, THE CHEEK, THE HIGH-PILED HEART AND THE SPINE, APPLAUSE, WE'VE GOT GIN AND GIN AND COLD WATER TO SOOTHE THE BLAZING SUNS OF OUR NIPPLES, WE LOOK UP INTO THE DARK SHAFT AND THE HORSES

SING, ADD AS TRUSTED SENDER, ADD AS UNTRUSTED SENDER, THE HAMMER, THE STIRRUP, THE BUS WINDOW, AND MACERATED, INFLAMED, ECZEMATOUS, PIGMENTED PLASTIC LIMBS, WE ARE THE POETIC PARAPHERNALIA OF THIS KITCHEN, BROKEN UP IN LIGHT AND REGENERATED IN DARKNESS, TRANQUILITY ITSELF AND NO RESISTANCE AND

BJØRN RASMUSSEN, born in 1983, debuted with *The Skin Is the Elastic Covering That Encases the Entire Body,* which was awarded several prizes, including the Montana Prize and the European Union Prize for Literature, and has been translated into seven languages. He has since published the novels *Decoration* and *Pregnant-ish,* and the poetry collection *Ming,* which was nominated for the Nordic Council's Literature Prize.

MARTIN AITKEN was a National Book Award finalist for his translation of Hanne Ørstavik's *Love,* and received the American-Scandinavian Foundation's Nadia Christensen Translation Prize in 2012. He has translated numerous books, including Dorthe Nors's *Karate Chop* and Helle Helle's *This Should Be Written in the Present Tense,* and he co-translated Karl Ove Knausgaard's *My Struggle: Book Six* with Don Bartlett.